A Blue Moon in August

a novel
by

Michael Lyons

Vol. 5 of the Sextet
My Years of Apprenticeship at Love

HiT MoteL Press
www.hitmotel.com

Copyright 2005 by Michael Lyons
All rights reserved.
First Edition

Library of Congress Cataloging in publication Data

Lyons, Michael
A Blue Moon in August
Vol. 5 of the Sextet *My Years of Apprenticeship at Love*
I. Title

ISBN: 0-9655842-5-9

Published by HiT MoteL Press

Designed by Michael Lyons

Urban Angst at the 7-11 in 2019 first appeared in *Puck, the Unofficial Journal of the Irrepressible*, Issue #10. Grateful acknowledgement is made to the editor Brian Clark. Also, thanks to proofreaders Regina Capurro, Eileen Key and Elizabeth Leonard.

To Father

. . . motherhood is a potent spell.
— Euripades . .

Table of Contents

Good-bye Bachelor Days

"Walker, I'm leaking." Sam looked scared. She had her hand on her pregnant tummy and was looking down at her pelvis. Her big brown doe-eyes were open round. "I've got a little spotting in my underwear, and I'm feeling really queasy."

"Well then. We better get to the hospital immediately," he said.

She called the day nurse, who called the on-call nurse, who called the advice nurse, who called the intern and eventually Walker and his sweet new wife Sam (Samantha Ann Majeweski)—he called her Sam for short—were making a hasty trip to the hospital for what they feared was a premature birth. Hustling and worried, they were out the door in no time flat. Walker drove them across town to the hospital in his ancient, ailing Mitsubishi Gallant with the stick shift.

On the way, they became stuck at the light on

Masonic for what seemed like an eternity. They had driven past the Haight-Ashbury, and were about to turn right and head down the hill to the emergency room at the sprawling Kaiser hospital facility. In that moment when events had conspired to hold them anxiously staring out the windshield, Walker felt the sobering portent of what was about to befall them set up a sense of inexorable inevitability in his mind. He realized he was passing through a portal into some kind of a "destiny zone." Though outwardly Walker gave the appearance of being a decent honest plugger, he knew this grew out of his being a perceiving rather than judging type—one who preferred to be surprised by events and did not usually take care of anything until it was thrust upon him. And now, not ten months into his first marriage, he was about to become a father. The change, from being a sex-obsessed procrastinator to a responsible dad with a new family, had to come in wrenching jerks—like the way a train starts up by the series of banging jolts that it passes along to the next car in succession—at discrete moments in time spread out over the nine month period one has to get ready for it. But was anyone ever ready for it? This was one of those profound moments of destiny lurching forward into the future.

Many times had the couple waited at this light; it had become a sort of transition point where they got serious about the hospital visit. Or the Lamaze class. Less than a month after the happy couple were back from their honeymoon in Hawaii—Sam took Walker to Hawaii for the first time (his sister had arranged a condo for them, on the 43rd floor, in the rarefied blue air overlooking the Honolulu yacht club)—Sam turned up pregnant. At their age, they thought it would take years; they were, after all, an older couple; Sam was forty-two. Friends had said: "At your age it will take at least a year to get pregnant." Not!! Walker had been looking forward to an extended honeymoon: he wanted to take time to get to know how to live together. It is quite a transition to go from being a bachelor able to crawl back into your own cave and dating when you wanted, to being a live-in, full-time husband. Being married is not so much romantic as it is nice and lovely. But Nooo. It was not to be. Fecund Hungarian (or is it the Italian?) will always out.

He had been both freaked out and delighted at the moment of truth when Samantha called him into the bathroom to witness the EPT error proof test. Sam's bright intelligent eyes were beaming with pride and excitement. The litmus paper had turned blue. Walker thought, Samantha is pregnant! EEEyooow, a baby! This is definitely going to make a man out of me. What he said was, "Great news! Strap on the seat belts. Ready or not. Here we go!"

So the new couple got to know each other making weekly trips over the hills of San Francisco to the great cosmogonical Kaiser hospital for prenatal check-ups and Lamaze classes. Going to Lamaze class is not the greatest way in the world to get to know your new bride. You have to openly discuss the sexual organs with people you barely know. They pass around a life-size plastic replica of the cervix. And you must keep your comments about camel-toe and calyx to yourself. You get to know the uterus so well you'd recognize one anywhere. Nurses recited the old wives' tales of water breaking, vaginal stress, hemorrhoids, and episiotomies which usually left Walker feeling humbled and generally queasy. But soon you get used to it.

Now, at the light, Sam was looking straight ahead out of the windshield with a glazed stare. Walker thought, she is probably cursing me right now for putting her through this. Or wondering, who I am.

Sam looked over at the man she had married and wondered what kind of father he would be. She had been trying to get him to see the work it involved—all the time involved—and he kept talking about all the fun things he was going to do with this child: chemistry sets, and studying integrated circuits and electronics projects and computer stuff together. He had talked about making animated story books in which the trees talked.

How had this man come into her life? He just strolled into her bookstore one day. It was in the ritzy Pacific Heights neighborhood of San Francisco. He was over there from Berkeley to visit one of the up-town shrinks. He was just strolling the safe avenues after his session, fresh and full of feelings, pumped up on the sense of identity you get when someone listens to you. He noticed the bookstore window had a display of Grateful Dead books: Brent the piano player had just died. Walker was excited about possibly encountering a book lover who was also a Deadhead. He entered the store and there he was: a tall, cool, drink of water in slacks and a seedy tweed sport coat that had suede elbow patches. He had fairly long hair, and the John Lennon glasses gave him an intelligent air. There she was, working behind the counter of her bookstore. The first thing he asked about, after he said Hi, was, "Do you still have the Good Night Moon Room?"

"Yes," she said, pleased. Smiling, "Want to see it?"

The woman behind the desk was attractive with long, dark hair that framed her wily face with a lushness which softened her penetrating dark eyes. As she led the way to the back of the book store he enjoyed watching her lustrous long, thick, dark hair sway back and forth, almost touching her shoulder blades.

She said, "The previous owners were gracious enough to let us keep it here. Lots of people still come to see it." Except, she thought, they weren't usually single men; they were usually moms pushing baby carriages. She noticed he had to duck under some low ceilings. "Mind your head here." She spoke up and introduced herself. "We just opened this store a couple of months ago. As you recall, it used to be all children's books. Now it is a general book store. My name is Samantha Majewski."

"My name is Walker Underwood," he said, nodding his head in respect. "Wow, there it is!" He stood before a life-size reconstruction of the Good Night Moon room, all green and dreamy and 3D like the way shadows play across a kid's mind in sleepy time. It had the big solid bed with the study arches and slats at the head and foot. A room built to look exactly like the green and blue child's room from the book, *Good Night Moon*, where a little baby bunny says good night to all the objects in its world.

She left to wait on a customer, and he wandered around the store among book cases everywhere. He browsed some of the shelves. He went back up to the front of the store near the light of the display window and started talking to her about the Grateful Dead books. "It's too bad about Brent."

"Yeah."

"I wonder who they will get to replace him?"

"He'll be hard to replace. That was one of the best incarnations of The Dead there ever was."

She seemed quite knowledgeable, even had some of the books authored by members of the band signed by them too. "Look at this," she said. And showed him a big picture book for children. "I got this one signed by Bob Weir. And Mickey Hart signed his book on drumming."

"Do you go to many shows?"

"Yes! I'm a Bluecoat. I work for Bill Graham Presents," she said. "I work in Rock Med too, at shows, a lot of times."

She invited him to stay. "Would you like some tea? I'm just boiling the water." She had a cozy little nook set up in the center of the store, with comfortable stuffed armchairs upholstered in a renaissance tableaux flower pattern.

"Wow, you don't see this in bookstores any more," he said.

"Well, I've always wanted to own a bookstore-café and do things my own way. It's still a dream. For my day job I work for the City. Yep, I'm one of Willie Brown's many minions." She opened up her tin of homemade cookies. She served him one on a little paper doily on a paper plate. Walker thought, at last, here she is: The girl who makes cookies to communicate.

He sat on the cushy armchair with the light of a floor lamp coming over his shoulder. He placed his mug of tea onto a coaster on top of a doily on a little round mahogany side table.

After that he lingered, pretending to browse the shelves. They engaged each other in more conversation.

When she went away to greet other customers, he found himself feeling a little possessive of her attention.

He visited her again the next day, and asked her out. They started dating. They were the nearly the same age. He made his move while on a stroll in North Beach, he kissed her in front of the great Tai Chi Dragon mural. They became lovers. Then he invited her into his past by showing her his album of childhood pictures. She showed him hers. Maybe it was because they were older and their biological clocks were going GONG, that the dating quickly took on an association of "commitment." Walker had always told himself he would wait until he was much older to get married, but he thought he better make his move before he was bedridden. And, as she was a high-energy, dark-haired, Italian-Hungarian beauty, he thought he could do with a bit of being bed ridden. Marriage seemed like a way to survive the AIDS epidemic decimating the kingdom. Moreover, even though they were older, they wanted to recreate family—something like the world you had when you were children.

At the unchanging light, she held her enormous spheroid stomach as it was thrashing and churning and said, "Damn I've never seen this trip take so long." She groaned then, and sighed—while at the exact same moment, the fog horns out in the bay sounded, and her sound got drowned into the louder blast, and they echoed each other. She noticed it too, and they looked at each other and laughed. He thought about the last sonogram made a few months back. That was the last time he had seen the little newt; actually the little newt was some what well-formed, kind of like Gumby. No doubt now much more humanoid. He wondered if they heard the sonogram in the womb. Some kind of huge ultrasonic sound storm for the womb-porpoise. Might be a good koan for meditation: Is the sonogram the first sound you hear? Vehicle within vehicle, carrier to convey—what. Then the light changed and their car moved on into the swirling vapor and shifting mists flowing with the traffic, as the fog horns of San Francisco bay—reverberating in the canyons of the city—sounded like some kind of giant spirit-chasing horns, blown by the protective deities of place, on a Tibetan mountain pass.

He pulled the car up at the front of the hospital under the overhead of the emergency entrance. He came around and helped Sam through the electric doors. To the guard he said, "I'll just be a moment," and helped her down the hall to the desk. He went off to park the car while she was admitted.

He found her again in the waiting room of the maternity ward on the fifth floor. It was just a few chairs set down in front of the elevator in a very public, heavily-trafficked place.

As they were sitting on the little felt-covered chairs, he reached over and took her hand, and he almost burst into tears, because they weren't ready. He thought, She is tired of being pregnant, but not ready to have this baby come outside her body yet and neither am I. And he said, "I'm really afraid for you and the kid, but it's you I'd hate to lose, because I love you, and the kid I don't even know yet. And I am just coming to know all your good, angelic, smart, funny, glamorous and other teen-appeal endearing qualities." He smoothed her hair, thinking, as he often did when he ran his fingers through her thick lustrous Hungarian hair, she could have been a model.

I keep trying to have these talks with her about how I am going to be a dad, about the vision of taking my kid down to see the ocean for the first time—the great wet mother of the gods—or about discovering the secrets of matter together doing kitchen chemistry and making horrible stinks, and she keeps getting really technical, about how I am skipping over the changing of the diapers. She is overly sober, always looking at the worst case scenario. She has us making out wills in the event we both die! No way! She is this high energy Aries, Italian/Hungarian. Dark, sturdy and smart. Her people are descended from Huns: live forever.

They finally admitted her into the delivery room, and they hooked her up to a bank of instruments beside a big sturdy bed with all kinds of mechanical settings. The bed had sides that went up and down, various leg holds and stirrups that pop up for delivery, and some way for the whole bottom half of the bed to pull away and drop down. The instruments had dials and monitors to track her contractions and the baby's heartbeat which the nurses at the front desk could watch. There was a tile bathroom off to the side. There was a chrome scrub sink for the doctors and nurses. The room was almost like a motel room, with a lot of TV sets and lights on poles. A nurse hooked up the needle for the IV, which connected to a bag of saline solution through a clear plastic hose. You could hear the baby's heart, amid all kinds of wooshes and whistles, gurgles and splashes, when he would kick and move around.

And Walker prayed to no one in particular: I . . .

and god damn, I wanted him to be OK, and not be born yet like other premature babies who have to be operated on, or whose lungs are not big enough to breath, and they have to start life in a respirator or whose hearing doesn't get finished and they end up deaf, and they never get properly bonded, or don't understand the world, or . . .

His wife was lying there hooked up to the machines, and Walker felt all this love for her. This motherly figure who until recently had been footloose and fancy free, and now has to live with the commitments. The one that made the compromises. Very touching, beautiful, warm, fleshy. Walker admired her courage. She could have used an IUD, but she didn't. We had faced that oracular moment blind, but together. That moment in which we decided to honor our commitment to each other. The decision could have been made or not made. The future is pregnant with possibilities, and like it or not we decide to cut that future off, or to go on with it. It's like stepping off into space. Walker thought, I'm the kind of person who does that, have done that all my life, but she isn't.

Here we are, he thought, a man and his wife, stuck together for a while. It takes a trip to the hospital for us to get face to face and talk. He began trying to pass the time and divert her misery by telling her stories and being charming. He told her about how he and his sisters used to play at being little savages and tribes-people. Being an only child Sam seemed to like stories about siblings. But she was very uncomfortable waiting for the doctor. Walker stepped out once when she had to use the bedpan. Finally, the doctor came in.

Then they did an ultrasound, and the couple could

see their baby in the uterus—in the womb, floating, stretching out his little legs, fast kicking around, maybe pushing off and floating across the screen. He was falling to them from a far off place, from a genetic pathway, from her people, Italian and Hungarian going back to the old country and his people, Scotch and Irish and French going back to the old country, and the lines going back and back, a pattern: the new being was flowing in, taking shape, little feet, little hands. Sam's doctor was a woman and she was very reassuring. She kept slithering the sound-wand around on Samantha's greased tummy to bring out the image of the baby. "There's his scrotum. Definite evidence he's a boy."

And it was awe-inspiring and horrendous and stupefying, and Walker didn't mean to appear confused, or dazed; but he wondered if the new being's psychological body was forming, and wondered about all the commitment it meant, and he was about to faint, thinking, I don't mean to appear reverent, dumfounded, or incapable, but I am.

There was this new, unborn face looking up—very beatific. Prominent eyes closed as though in pain or ecstasy or deep heartfelt understanding. Because there was no fat on the face you could see the bone structure, the face looked like what it might look like when he got older. For a moment, the face reminded Walker of the ancient tanned, metallic face of one of the Bog People, those people who had been thrown into the British peat bogs as a sacrifice to the gods—they were dug up—their mummies preserved by being tanned in the bog fluid—folded up in fetal position. In the black and white sonogram, the little body shapes were dark against white amniotic fluid. It was bathed in a cone of light, reflecting the cone of sound, the spotlight of sound. And because the sound was bouncing into his slightly open mouth, the image in the screen made his mouth look like it was emitting light.

And his nose. . . "He's good looking!" Walker said. "He's got your aquiline nose. Thank God he doesn't have mine."

The Entity looked a little troubled and twisted, as though he were looking up at them from a watery grave where he had been for thousands of years, and Walker wondered what he felt floating there, being maybe half-porpoise, half-whale, with the life-line going from there to his mother, all the way back to creativity in the water. He looked so content, like an enraptured saint might look, meeting God. It made Walker wonder, What lifeline do I have going from me; in what water am I flowing?

And on the monitor all the pens were keeping track of the baby's heart and of the contracting. And sure enough, there were contractions, about ten minutes apart. Small but regular, and Walker thought, "Hello babe, good by bachelor ways. / Are you getting tired of waiting, stay a bunch more days. / We're not ready for you, you're too little, not far enough along. / This married life is giving me hope, so I say / good-by bachelor ways."

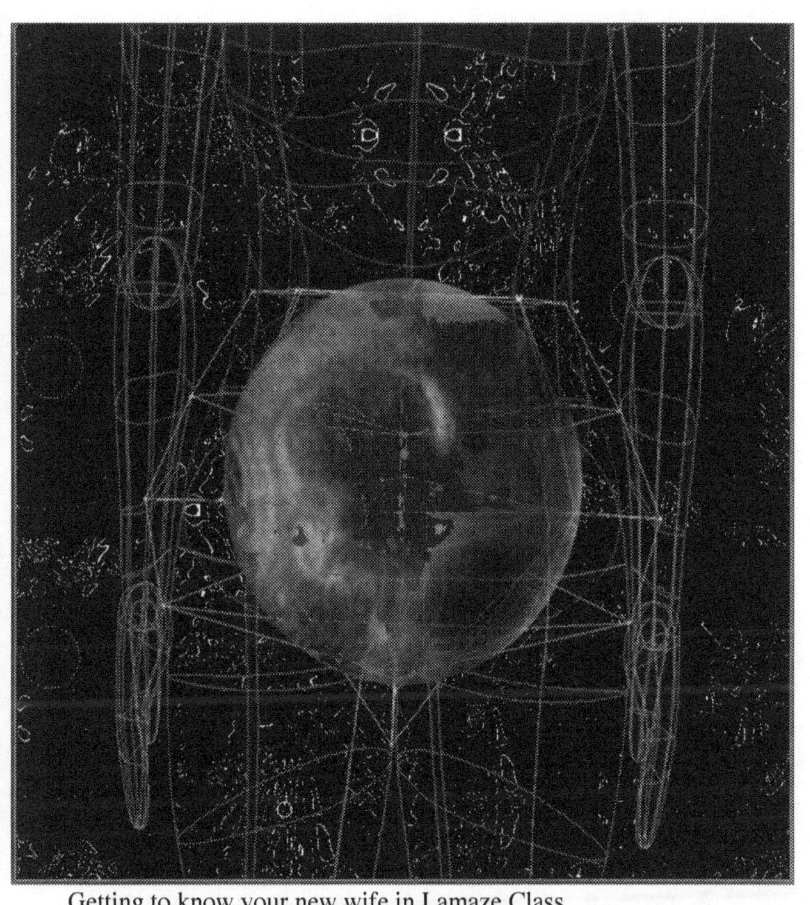

Getting to know your new wife in Lamaze Class

Pandit

After seeing Sam into her room at the hospital, Walker went back to their condo to get her a few things—her hair brush, her glasses, her tooth brush, and he found himself walking around looking for her socks. He looked into her drawers; she had given him a drawer in her dresser. Then he started looking in her huge walk-in closet and he realized, I don't even know where she keeps her socks! And his bewilderment deepened. I don't really know very much about her at all. It was ghostly and lonely in the house without her, and he kept thinking about how little he knew her. And how little she knew of him. He got her gym bag and her travel kit. A travel kit. Isn't that just like her to have everything neat and all arranged?

As he passed by his own disorganized office-room he thought, Isn't it about time I cleaned up my room, where every horizontal surface is covered with papers, and books, and juggling balls, and discs, and tapes, as though I were trying to control the flow of time, to slow time down, to capture it a bit, and it's all just going by so fast. He felt a strong pull of longing to pick up the tenants of the story he was working on. What was it? About this guy who had invented his own zodiac, his own time. It was pretty much of a downer. Some of the signs in the new zodiac were Hypodermic Needle about the narcotic effect of modern life. And Droid, a comment on the modern worker. Walker himself was born under the sign of Bimbo, which was unlike Droid in that it had a choice about how to prostitute itself with work. Though kind of cynical, exploring the idea of people as meat puppets, it was an exercise in mythopoeisis. But with the new developments in his life, the new hope, he was leaving the negativity behind and was having trouble getting on in this story.

Anyway, he told himself, I can't get into that now. He remembered the "chat" she had given him about "his" room where he had his computers and printers from Berkeley and his futon bed. I agreed to start working on cleaning it out so we can start the nursery. I suggested that I look for an office, a little studio office to rent somewhere in the neighborhood. I hated this neighborhood, it is full of crack dealers. It's about time I got organized, and got ready for this kid, and get him moved into something in the country because he deserves it. Get him out of this place where the people are so angry they just toss their cheeseburger wrappers on the sidewalk and walk away. . . She has done so much to prepare for this baby and what have *I* done? But sometimes she drives me nuts with all this nesting behavior. She is like Martha Stewart on speed! You have to be careful what you say to her. Like the time she asked me if I liked a pattern in the stoneware and I said I liked the simple one with the blue band. Couple of weeks later, boxes of the stuff—enough to seat a dozen people—show up. She asked me, "What do you think about a blue nursery? I am going to decorate the nursery in safari/jungle, but I hate to paint the walls brown or olive drab."

This was before we knew it was a boy—though I was SURE it was a boy, and I said, "OK."

"Well, we better paint it pink," she said. "Then, for sure—it will be a boy."

She was almost finished painting in the hall and bathroom when I came home the other day. I had to get on her case about paint fumes and take the paint brush from her hand and finish the wall myself. Then later she was on the phone to Joan, her wild heavy-drinking good-ole-girl friend, who has a young daughter. Sam said, "I committed the mortal sin of painting while pregnant! Walker lectured me! I had every single window in the house opened, and I was just doing the edges when he TOOK the paintbrush away from me. Wow, I feel like a princess. Can I be pregnant all the time? No painting, no litter box."

He wandered back into their room, and noticed the sides and ends of a crib stacked against a wall. I haven't even put together the crib yet. Luckily she got it used, it is very nice wood. He saw himself in the big mirror over the dresser. Alone with his thoughts he could be himself. There I am, basically a bohemian, a white-shirt, blue-jean (southern collegiate style) bohemian who, because of good manners, presented well. He was what the women his age called "a diamond in the rough." Rough is right. He cringed thinking about his funky car. Sam had thought he had a nice new car, but that one was just a rental he had for a contract job. She was surprised his own set of wheels was a wretched seven-year-old Mitsubishi. I bought it used; never owned a new car in my life. It was the only Japanese import I can fit into. Besides, a car is just transportation anyway. But it was really horrible that night in North Beach when it wouldn't start. We had to sit there—Sam as big as a house, in front of a Chinese food restaurant—waiting, for a vapor lock to unblock or something. What if that had happened on the way over to the hospital?!

He got her a piece of pie, a pie she had baked for their evening out. He put it into one of the little pie shaped Tupperware containers. He smiled at how uncivilized he was before he met her: I didn't even know about burping Tupperware. And he thought, I deserve this child. And I am giving myself this. And he is going to sing to me, and come and tell me about the NEW quantum electrodynamics, and I'm going to try not to be so far out of it that I can't understand it, or that our relationship would be so bad that he wouldn't care to talk to me anyway.

When Walker got back to the hospital, they had moved Sam into a more comfortable room. He placed her novel and sweets on her bed and got her settled. And they were just sitting around reading, hoping it was only false labor—Braxton Hicks contractions that may start out strong, but taper off and then stop after a while.

Later in the night, a nurse from India came into the room. Walker imagined his wife was getting tired of this and could use some distraction. He decided to engage this Indian nurse in conversation. Since he had a friend in India at the time who was studying mandalas with the Dalai Lama at the Dharmasala at Macleodgange, he asked the nurse if she had ever been to Macleodgange.

She thought for a minute and said, "No, I've never heard of it."

"It's where the Dharmasala is. Where the Dalai Lama lives."

"The Dalai Lama lives in Tibet," she said.

Walker realized she was probably out of touch, for the Dalai Lama had lived in India since fleeing Tibet ahead of the Chinese in 1949, but then she said, "The Dharmasala is the general name for like a monastery or a church; it is a place where monks live."

They got to talking about priests and religion. Walker drew out the nurse to talk about astrology, and she really perked up. He wanted to understand something of how a person from this ancient culture—a place where they really believed in astrology, are perhaps ridden with horoscope—understood the world.

The Nurse spoke in an Indian-English accent, "You know, they have these men there, at the Dharmasala, and they are truth-sayers, like priests, and they are called Pandits, and they spend all their time in prayer. They lead a very simple life, they don't ask for anything, and they are not into the material world. All they want to be is truth sayers. And when my husband and my father went to see one he said, 'You will have a son in America.' And we were shocked. And it was true. Here we are in America, and we have a child born here. And when I went to see them they had many, many books on their shelves. And another one, when he read my palms, he looked at the lines of my children, and saw that the line for the female child was not long-lived, and sure enough I have had a miscarriage of the girl. And there was a line of one of the boys that was cut off, and it is true that I have had an abortion. He could read all that in my palm. . . We believe very much in the horoscope."

Walker thought that was all right. After the Indian nurse left, he and Sam got into a discussion of astrology. He said, "You need to know the sun sign, the rising sign and the moon sign, right?"

Sam said, "Everybody in my generation has, at one time or another, looked into it."

"Especially as it was something that interested Jung." Walker added. "I think it's OK to believe in astrology. I mean it doesn't contradict any physical laws. Gravity gives us plenty of experience believing in transparent forces that you could not see except for when it was acting on something, like a ball falling off the table for example. And gravity influences everything, shaping the physical world. Perhaps astrology is a kind of primitive psychological gravity impacting all the things in the universe. Certainly the planets do put some kind of spin on that force."

And then to pass the time, he put on an Indian-English accent and went into his storyteller mode: "Although it was all laid out, a long time ago, when they thought the sun was the center, and thus you had the sun was rising, or the moon was rising, around the earth. . .

(Here the storyteller designates a great arch in the sky indicating the celestial sphere.)

"And I think of it now in a more humanistic way, for one thing it is an artifact of man's greatest hubris to project his mental functioning out there on the ecliptic, the furthermost point of what he can see with his naked eye. The ecliptic is the projection of the equator out into infinity and can be seen from all over the world. And at night the sky seems to rotate from west to east, and along the ecliptic, you have the animals, the zodiac. I mean different people see different things out there, but it was basically the ancient Greek shepherds who worked this all out, and it was their world of goats, and bulls, and lions and scorpions, and beautiful maidens bringing the harvest of food in, and carrying water, and catching fish.

"And they made these charts by drawing a circle with these animals of the zodiac all around it. And it was a very big part of their life. They looked for the sign of the ram when it was time to plant in the spring, and they marked the solstices and equinoxes from it. Even the names of our days, Monday is Moonday, Saturday is Saturnday, Sunday is Sunday."

Soon the contractions had subsided, but they kept Sam in overnight anyway for observation. Him they sent home. Her they let out the next day. It was a Sunday.

Three Body, small
2
-2
2
name m x y vy ax ay
sun 50 .000 .000 .000 .000 0.023
moon 1 -1.391 4.130 2.433 0.425
mars .01 106.425 -4.911 0.001
Clear
constants
G: 1
Scale: 32
dt: 0.05
xOff: 256
yOff: 256

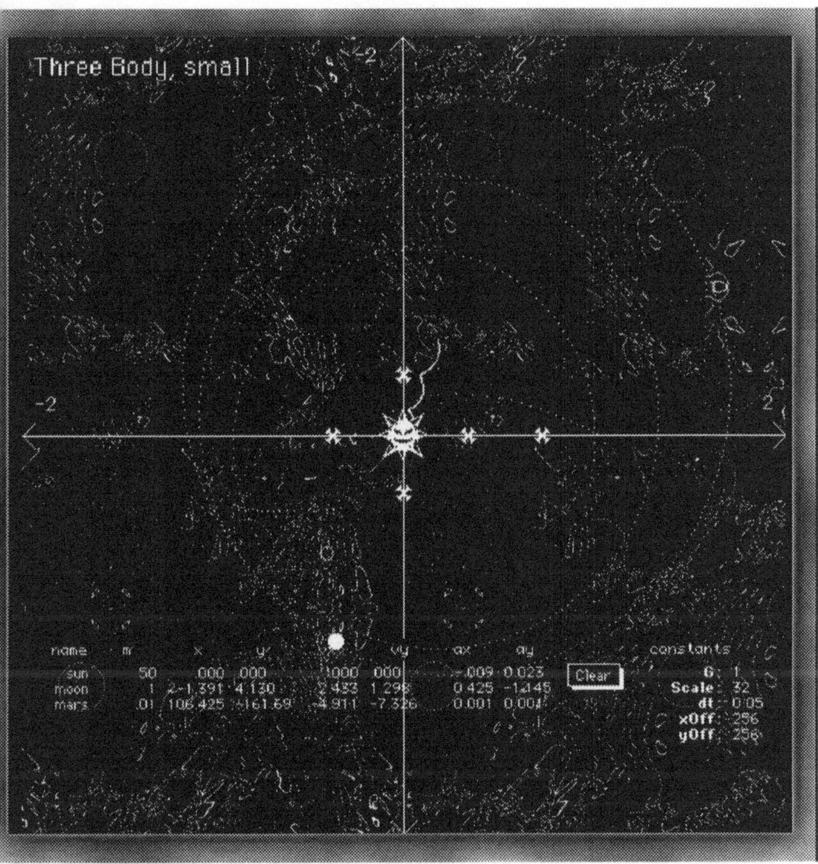

Nativity

Expanding the Nest

Walker picked up Sam from the hospital and they trudged up a hill to where he parked the car. They drove back to their neighborhood kind of freaked out, quiet, looking straight ahead. As usual the streets of their neighborhood were infested with crack dealers—moved by police over the hill from the projects. All up and down the streets you had these black guys standing around flashing their wide open loitering eyes, looking into the low-rider cars going by. They were always talking on cell phones.

Walker said, "I'll probably be the last person on earth to get a cell phone."

She said, "These guys are the early adopters of new technology."

Sam was cool. His age. Similar background. Had good hippie aspects. Can talk. Can smoke weed with her. That had helped them get close. He said, "Yeah, I got to encounter one of them the other day when I took the BART and the streetcar back from Berkeley. I was walking up our street and there her was! Standing on the corner in the shadow under a street light: this big spade dude. He's got a beer can in a small paper bag. He was grinning sheepishly, working his mouth around in an O—kind of like Death sucking on a life saver. And the guy says to me: 'Need some rock? Got all kinds of rock. $5, $10, $25.'"

As soon as they got into their little condo and Sam was settled in, she got on the phone and started calling her network of woman friends. Even though Sam was an only child, and didn't have any sisters and cousins close by, she had an extensive network of female friends. She was going to be an older mom; so were a lot of women in her generation.

She called her good running-buddy Joan, who had a four-year-old daughter. "Hey, Joan. What's up?"

"Not much."

"Well I just got back from spending the night in the hospital! It was a false labor! Walker took me over Saturday night. Boy was I scared. And we had a sonogram and I saw that it was a boy!"

"It's a boy!?"

"Yep, it's a boy."

"Cool."

"We are really delighted."

"They're a lot less trouble than girls."

"Yeah. . . . Man. We are not ready."

"Tell me about it. Whoever was ever ready?"

"I've got a lot more work to do on our nursery. And I've got to get some more baby clothes."

"Well, I can't help you there. Those days are in the past for me."

"Unfortunately, everyone must have gotten rid of their baby stuff last year! But I did find some really cute baby clothes."

"What baby clothes aren't cute, right?"

"Yeah, right. But I even bought some little girl clothes! I told Walker that the only reason I bought the girl stuff is that if I hadn't bought it, we would have a girl. So I bought the girl stuff, so we will have a boy. Honestly, though, we would have been just fine if we were having a girl. In fact, I like some of the girl names we picked much better than boy names."

Yeah, the boy's names are pretty plain. John and Mark, . . .

"Luke and Matthew. Walker wants to call him Shredder, isn't that funny?"

"Why?"

"Why that? I don't know. He thinks he is going to tear things up, I guess."

Sam said, "I've got to find a bigger bra. My tits are getting huge!" She whispers to Joan on the phone: "I've noticed Walker looking at me."

"Men like big tits."

"And mine are getting huge. Ha ha."

Then she was off the phone in a mad search through her drawers for her pregnancy bra. She remembers that she has not put away laundry done before trip to maternity ward. It is still stuffed in the dryer basket in the garage. Sends Walker out to get it. "Bring up the whole basket, would you, honey?" After he emptied the dryer into a basket and brought the basket to her, she fished in and plucked out the large cotton bra and held up her prize. Then she set about folding the rest of her clean clothes and put them away. She had to admit if felt pretty good to be married and to be off on this new adventure. Can't knock it.

Breeding females begin to widen their nest. It's a biological imperative. Samantha started going on about the baby's room: "You said you were going to do something about clearing out the room for a nursery."

Walker said *(a little peeved)*: "Well, yes. We don't have to do it immediately. The baby will bunk it with us until he is a little older. Meanwhile I'm *looking* for an office."

She said, "Well it would be good for the tax situation. You can write it off."

He said, "Yep. I might be able to rent a room in a house in the neighborhood. Yes, I'll start to look for a room in a nearby house."

He looked at her with love.

It is true that she did, or used to, get him very excited, he had her and the memories, the scenes of their lovemaking to keep him inspired.

Marriage felt like a culmination of the many attempts at living together with girlfriends. He had embarked upon several in the serial monogamies of his 20s and 30s. But this was different. For now he had given his word, had put the full weight of commitment into this marriage business, and as much as anything it was a commitment to himself.

It was a graduation and celebration of all the sweet, and not so sweet women he had been with and who had been warm and talked with him and slept with him in the night. And the time he has spent with them *was* sweet for the most part. Perhaps some had even loved him. Maybe she loved him.

And he felt so much love and tenderness toward her beautiful brunette self, and they used to make things really hot for each other but now they were off on another project.

He said, "Don't worry about it. I'm taking care of you. I've got your back. . . . What are we going to call this critter anyway."

The Prowess of Kong

Feeling a little bit "pushed out of the nest," Walker found himself reaffirming his stance on commitment. Walker knew he wanted to become a father, of that he was certain. But it was for a strange reason: it was a Buddhist thing; he wanted to have his generosity tested, and rise to the occasion. And he wanted to experience parental love, as he thought it might be the closest thing to Bodhichitta he'd ever have in his life. He just knew that becoming a parent would teach him a lot about love. And life. And he wanted the sense of commitment to the age. He wanted to truly pass something on to the next generation.

Walker's ideas on marriage were formed from living in a tantric Buddhist commune. These theoretical ideas were quite different from the standard-issue American marriage. It took a brush with death to push Walker back over the edge into traditional marriage. The moment of decision occurred on a trip up to the commune land with his *compadre* Kevin Phelan.

Walker and Kevin, or KP as they called him, had become friends when, some seven years earlier, they had been husbands in a group marriage commune of experimental living, called prosaically enough—the House. (It had a Buddhist name, the Sangha of Dorje Chang.) He and KP had exposed themselves to, and weathered, a lot of psychological drama stuff together. So when Walker was wrestling with the decision to start living with Sam and maybe even marry, he was glad for the invitation to spend a long weekend on the commune land, to gain some clarity in his thinking about where this latest love was going. Nothing like a surfeit of fresh air and physical labor to set the mind straight. The land that the House owned was being sold, and KP and Walker were going up to do some cleanup work. The plan was to share the driving and get all the way up across the boarder into Oregon that night and get a motel in Ashland. And it was on this trip that Walker gave up the ideal of the commune and decided to try good old American marriage with Sam.

The land was 340 acres near Mount Shasta that the House had acquired to try their mettle on. Situated just on the California side of the Oregon border, it consisted of over a half mile of long sloping valley including its ridge tops. This valley had a stream running down the center of it, drawing and holding life, and emptying into a pond at the bottom of the land. Chase had created the commune that they just called simply, the House. It flourished through the 70's but despite a valiant effort to keep things going, disbanded after Chase's death in 1983. The House was survived by the miracle of many lifelong attachments, some marriages and the land—which was now to be turned over to a nature conservancy.

Even though the main reason Walker had gone on the cleanup trip was to get some input from his trusted friend, he was cautious bringing it up. Having an ulterior motive made him feel kind of awkward at first when KP picked him up in Berkeley after work Friday and they set off for the Labor Day weekend. So while KP did the driving up interstate I-5, Walker bided his time, looking for the right moment. But so far on this trip Walker seemed to be talking only when KP wasn't listening. All the way up KP was busy pondering the logistics of the cleanup. He plotted out loud various scenarios of pulling a trailer. He planned the schedule. He worked out the best attack for making two trips to the dump on Sunday. Walker finally was able to bring up his concern in a roadside diner. It was past midnight and starting to rain when they got to Redding and decided to change drivers. KP pulled his black Saab off Interstate-5 into the parking lot of a truck-stop. The place was packed so he found a parking spot two rows away from the entrance to the bright stainless steel diner. KP proceeded to dig his grungy good-ole-boy Budweiser cap out of the leather door-panel pocket and put it on with a flourish and tug of the bill. He looked across the bucket seat to Walker, a sly grin on his otherwise serious, bearded face.

Walker was delighted to see the hat. "Say, Bud, I haven't seen that hat since the last time we were up here." Walker remembered then, the last time when they had pitched their two tents at the top of what they called Chase's Peak, the highest point on the land, in the waving green grass of that sandy-colored rock outcropping. And across the valley, way off in the distance, dominating the terrain for 100 miles around, you could see the massive upheaval of Mount Shasta rising alone out of the plane of the central valley. A single peak, piercing the cobalt-blue high-altitude sky.

"Yep. Gotta keep the rain out muh face," Kevin Phelan drawled in his best imitation redneck accent (which was pretty funny coming from under his Scottish brogue).

"Man, I'd of thought it would have deteriorated by now after five years," Walker said as he dug a white rangers cap, one like they wore in Viet Nam, out of his small pack. He liked it because it was indestructible, it could be crushed in a knapsack, it floats, and was made of natural cotton. He did tuck its string up under its crown, for it wouldn't do to be unduly noticed by the locals. Moving side by side through a drizzle, the two tall, slightly-overweight men loped quickly across the busy, bright, middle-of-the-night parking lot. Upon going through the glass door into the diner, they took their hats off. There was quite a crowd of burly truckers sprawled out in their own section of the noisy restaurant. Try as he might to look like one of the locals, KP's carriage and demeanor was European-born aristocrat—authoritative. Walker's gangly, anxious-to-please, nervous affability made him appear the younger of the two, though he was older by nine years and even taller.

Walker—juiced from being on the road again—found himself feeling expansive amid the clatter of a middle-America truck stop. Spreading his arms out in the booth and smiling at KP across the formica table, he almost shouted above the din of the noisy diner, "Yay!

Don't it feel good to be on the road, again? I'm gonna order coffee and apple pie!" A waitress wearing a pink uniform with a starched white blouse took their order.

Walker wanted to take the opportunity of being face to face in the restaurant with KP to get into a serious conversation with him. On the way up, Walker had been trying to talk about his relationship with this new woman he was in hot pursuit of. Things were getting frightfully serious. In times past, the two men, had been able to talk about anything.

"Man, I need a reality check," Walker started in. "I really like this woman Samantha I'm going out with. I'm thinking of asking her to start living together! It's way past time I give up this bachelor living. . . But I don't know, man. I've been living alone for so long. I like being able to shift for myself. But it's getting to feel weird though, an unmarried guy, over forty, living alone in the San Francisco Bay area. My parents—I can just FEEL my mother's imagination running away with her and them getting suspicious that I'm gay."

KP got an exasperated look on his face as if to say: We are not supposed to be driven around by our mother's fears.

Walker duly noticed it and continued: "This gal is really different from me, man. She's into politics; even walks the precincts, for Christ's sake. She showed me this picture of her going back twenty years, in the 70's, that she cut out of the Chronicle. She's in this little miniskirt, man, this little suede miniskirt—with pleats! Looking so *fine*. Walking a precinct! Probably in some tough neighborhood. I mean, I'd never do anything like that."

Walker imagined himself looking out of one of the

tenement windows at this dark-eyed young beauty whose big caring heart had her out there doing what she believed would help the world. Made him love her even more. And he loved little pleated skirts on women. Probably a throwback to his years in Catholic grade school.

KP, who had met Sam once, said, “She looks a lot like Dahlia.”

Oooo, this was a stab in the heart. Dahlia had been Walker’s great love in the House. Dahlia had once actually been married to KP, a marriage arranged by Chase to help KP stay in the House. Though KP was too polite, out of deference to Walker’s great obsession over her, to go into detail, they had shared an appreciation of Dahlia’s good looks. That made them blood brothers, brothers-in-law or brothers-of-the flesh. But that was long ago when they had been part of the great experiment. Now Dahlia had married her main man from the House and had a kid. “Well yeah, you know, that’s my type,” said Walker. “I love tall, handsome, dark-haired women.”

Walker continued extolling the virtues of his new love. “And she’s got a voice, man. Goes to church every Sunday, sings in the choir. And, and . . . she’s a entrepreneur, got her own business.”

KP asked, “Well? What does she think about it?”

“About what?” asked Walker.

“About where the *relationship* is going,” KP said. He said this in a teasing, valley-girl tone, making fun of the way girls are always analyzing and to hurry Walker out of his tendency for evasiveness in psychological matters.

“Well, I don’t know. She said something to the

effect that we both have lived with people in the past, and it is easy to get out of that and she needed more commitment."

"Ah yes," KP said, thoughtfully. He raised and lowered his eyebrows to comical effect. "Commitment." He paused for dramatical effect. "Of course you know, this means *marriage.*" He seized on the word, as though he were going into shock.

"Eeeeeeyowwwww!" Walker moaned. "Marriage. I'm afraid you're right."

KP paused and looked thoughtful for a moment. "What do I know? Lucia and I aren't married. But I'd say it would be good for *you.* You need more commitment in your life. Get married." He looked at his friend in all seriousness. "And buy a house. That'll help you keep your job."

Then KP added, as though it were an afterthought off the top of his head: "Have a kid too, that will help with your stability problems. Take them on as a yoga." KP gave Walker a that'll-settle-your-hash look. They both laughed.

After that, KP pulled out a pen and started making lists with boxes and flow charts on his paper napkin of things to do at the cleanup. "We'll get a twenty-foot trailer and pull it behind Kong. We'll gather together enough stuff for two loads and get it all piled up on Saturday. Then we'll load up Kong with a load on Saturday night. We'll take the first load to the dump on Sunday, then come back and take another load."

Kong is a 4-wheel drive, 1 1/2 ton JEEP pickup with two speed real axle. It was on loan from the new owner, a friend of the House. Kong is perfectly adapted to the environment of the Siskyou mountains around Mount

Shasta. When the House bought Kong, the beast was already famous in these parts for its prowess in tractor pull contests. Kong was its stage name.

As they got up to leave, KP tucked the napkin notes into his pocket. Outside he gave the keys to Walker, who took over the driver duties. Back on the road KP slept, and Walker was left alone with his thoughts. He felt kind of dismissed. It used to be in the House that people gave each other good attention. Come to think of it, that was not always true. He had to laugh at his plight though—turning over and over in his mind, the classic question: "Should I marry?" What did I expect from KP? We had both been married before into the same group marriage. That's what the House was. The idea of contemplating standard monogamous marriage as opposed to "polyfidelity," was a foreign heresy there. This is a question only I can answer.

Walker respected his friend's advice and treasured the confidences that they shared, yet he had a different set of loyalties now. AIDS was raging outside in the kingdom and the yuppies pulled in and made provisions enough that they do not need to be out there in the petri-dish mosh-pit of dating. In 1990 it looked like marriage and low-tech cocooning with the family was a good defense against fatal VD.

After an obligatory smoke in Weed, California they swapped driving shifts again. KP grinned as he slid the cover over the bowl of his pipe with one hand and smoothly put it away into an inside pocket of his vest. "This will help me navigate this last twisty turny bit here before the border."

Once they were underway Walker said, "Man I'm glad we have Kong to do all this work."

"Yeah, me too. What we really need is Robo-Kong."

Walker said, "You know I saw *King* Kong on T.V. again recently. It's pretty good. It's kind of film noir crossed with a sci-fi. It's black and white and dark and faded. It's kind of like a dream, they go back into time and see all these ancient monsters, like dredging up pictures of the ancient reptilian back brain, where there is only fighting over territory and fate. Of course it is very racist too. Remember where the Kong grinds down these black natives into the mud?"

"Yeah, that's right," KP replied.

"It was made during the great depression of the 30's," Walker said. "Did you know it was an *allegory* for those bad economic times? That's right. We talked about it in a film class I took once in college. Kong is a metaphor for the bad economy. Remember the beginning? This guy wants a girl for his movie so he goes to the Woman's Mission where he sees some pretty hard-looking cases. He finally gets Fay Ray by saving her from some irate shop keeper because she was about to steal an apple. People like King Kong, they like to see his rage, like where he tears up the subway, because they get to have revenge against an economy that has abandoned them. And you notice Kong has no family. He's alone. He's the only one of his kind. Where is Kong's mother? She has abandoned him."

"Hmm," said KP. "So now, the next thing you'll tell me is that Kong represents pre-oedipal rage."

"That's right!"

"Pretty far fetched."

"It's true... it's really true," Walker said, as he closed his eyes and drifted off.

As Walker and KP settled into the quiet of a midnight drive for the long stretch, their minds cruised. Walker thought KP looked possibly a little contrite for being kind of short with him back in the truck stop. It was the *roles* they kept getting into around each other—KP was the responsible one, even though Walker was the same age as KP's older brother! Still, it had been contemptuous. Boy, in the heyday of the House, people would have got on his case for not being able to pay attention. Walker had to smile as he remembered that on these trips up to the land they were in *group*, and people were expected to be deadly serious. It was as if whenever two or more House people are gathered together there also is Group Mind. He pictured the House as they were massing, outside their building in the Mission—a bunch of gypsies getting ready to caravan out of town in a fleet of rented sedans. The House made the trip from their penthouse in the Mission driving the five hundred miles up to the land every Friday night, coming back Sunday, one group per car. It was serious group work all the way up and serious group work all the way back. Walker shook his head in disbelief: it was amazing we didn't draw any more attention to ourselves than we did. It was because there was a lot of activity in and out of the building and the parking lot. And the Mission is a colorful place. Still, people might have noticed us in the way the women were. The House women walked with a looseness in their hips, like native women, so forceful, hard working, totally secure with all the House brothers around. The House was a group marriage / tantric religious cult—a sangha.

Walker pictured the slender, strong form of Dahlia coming down the stairway from the loft, proud and going outside. Loose and easy in their saunter the wild women of the House, walking out into the Mission while city dwelling commuters, trapped, hunched over their steering wheels, glanced out their passing car windows and looked on with interest. In the House you were always being watched over by your friends: people who were on the same path as you, people to whom you were married.

In his mind Walker zoomed up the last flight of stairs, through a single door, into the penthouse. It was one large room, with a floor dividing it into above and below. He had spent many a night in fear and love, looking up at the rafters holding up the floor of that loft. At night the forty or so adults rolled out futons on the floor right side by side, downstairs and upstairs, for sleeping and love-making.

KP slowed the car's speed as he passed a big rig going the other way on a curve through the mountains. He checked the speedometer and other lighted gauges displayed in a neatly curved dashboard. He loved the Saab cockpit with its leather seats and all its round gauges like clocks with little lighted numbers transducing the functions of motion.

Walker felt both the peril of night driving and his trust in KP, who even though he was slightly stoned, was always a paragon of responsibility. In the concentric scattering of light from the headlight of an oncoming car on the wet windshield, Walker saw the circular symmetry of a tanka. This drew his mind's attention back into the House. Sitting. In meditation. In front of a window, a stained glass window? No, it was one of the tankas. Of course! How could he forget the gallery of tanka paintings hanging on the walls downstairs. They were on each of the four walls. These priceless, consecrated, sacred, tanka paintings from Tibet made the House a temple. Some were sometimes veiled and sometimes unveiled, and people were directed to sit and meditate in front of them. They were doors of perception to a gone world. It all came back to him. As another car wooshed by in the opposite direction, the force of its shock wave spreading the water drops on their own windshield so that the oncoming car's headlight beams were dispersed in radial groupings, he thought about the synesthesia of the colors. They almost made the paintings have sounds, you could hear the loud horns and gongs and deep base vibration of the chanting, contemplating monks. The House did a lot of chanting. Their Buddhism was some kind of hybrid cross of Zen and Pure Land. Zen for its no-nonsense sitting, and Pure Land in that they tried to be conscious at all times, and had rituals to help them stay in that focus.

These paintings were steeped in bioenergy; it gave them an aurora. They were a riotous orgy of colors, yet flat and iconographic: rivers flowing into land, and usually a mountain—a fountain, an abundance of energy streaming out from a fortress isle, or a four-sided platonic monastery. The monastery at the center of the painting represented the Self, and the figures, the monsters—my God the monstrous figures, thought Walker. There was nothing in the west like them. The west, who was there in western art who ever went after these subjects? Bosch, yes, and the early religious painters, patronized by the Catholic church. They painted beautiful haloes. But the tankas were about bioenergy streaming out of the painting at the viewer. And the Mahakalas, big black Mahakalas with bulging eyes dancing on corpses. Or the wrathful deities, horrific, bearded—some actually looked human except they had fiery orange hair. The corpses were depicted with such nacreous, lily-white, night-shades. The indigenous people of the world did not hide themselves from Death. But these pictures of walking corpses were symbolic pictures of the Hungry Ghost. Yes. That's what they were. Chase had helped them understand it was a picture of dependency, the root of all suffering.

As the dark shapes of hills and rivers raced past the moving car, Walker wondered if he too had become a Hungry Ghost with the long neck and its closed throat, the barracuda jaws (the power underbite), and an obsession with control. You get a bloated belly and are soft in the middle, you have a pencil thin neck with which to feed that great insatiable hunger. This resulted in a kind of confusion of meaninglessness and ennui, a lack of imagination, a vacuum of envy that sought to fill the void with work, sex, entertainment. Chase saw the yuppies as trying to fill this void in values by constantly buying the next thing—an obsession with objects and owning them.

The western mind leads to material greatness and to spiritual poverty. Of course there were other names for it, neurosis, psychosis, obsessive compulsive syndrome. Civilization and its discontents. Urban angst. Alienation. Chase saw dependency as *the* plague of modern time. Chase had created the House as an ongoing confrontation to, and treatment of, the Hungry Ghost syndrome. He got the treatment from the same ancient sources he got this name for it, from his reading in Buddhist religions and art.

And by god those monks were right. After ten years of meditation, group sex, psychotherapy, and LSD nearly every weekend, the western reality construct of constant war between the super-ego and the self seemed to recede way into the back of my mind, and those internal lights—call them insights, bioenergy halo, auras, beatific states, chakras, Kundalani or whatever—started looking good to me. Now after 5 years away from it I can't believe I am such a techie in spite of all that. I'd still just as soon seek the inner light—except I don't want to end up broke when I'm old and be a burden to anybody. *Great choice in life.* Always the extreme tension between being and having. It had been good, though, to get stoned and contemplate the iconography of the tankas. The tankas were a kind of vehicle for carrying the mind into another world. All their philosophy was there. It was the story of the journey of a soul being shocked awake and being killed and reborn many times and being possessed of demons and somehow working your way toward liberation. Buddhism taught that liberation from all forms of dependency is the path to freedom. You had to make yourself a real person. To be a person that pursued the inner light, you had to make yourself as an instrument of the light. There are stranger things on this earth then man has ever thought, certainly western man.

The tanka canvases luffed as he turned his contemplation into the memories of everyday life in the commune and lifted his gaze to float about the loft. He saw downstairs: the two doors to the unisex bathrooms and showers. He saw the large communal vegetarian kitchen.

In the group marriage, you were supposed to be at group every night after dinner. Walker started flashing pictures in his mind: speeded-up, time-elapsed photos. He could see the ritual of people's lives. Several people came home from work at once and he could simultaneously follow each one of them as they change out of their suits, get into their chores, take care of the plants, sit in group. It was as though he were floating above it, and the paths of motion of the House people had accelerated so fast that the blur of their motion froze into a still picture of the trajectory of their lives in the House. This frieze of order that modulated the myriad activities of the house was ritual. So that even though they led very chaotic lives in the city, there was so much ritual, and sameness about their daily schedule, that work and relationship became as all one thing flowing together into psychology or religion.

The futons were neatly rolled and stored upstairs in a great pile, back by where the pipes came through and made it impossible to stand up. In his mind Walker zoomed to the back of the loft where there were rows of closets. Imagine only being allowed personal possessions that could be kept in a two-foot wide closet space—all that was allotted to each person. The dwelling of the House, the Loft was a compassion compression chamber. That's what it was, an endless slumber party from hell inside a submarine on top of a building in a penthouse. Walker smiled to himself. That's why we were so grateful to get out of that pressure cooker and get onto the land. Chase had fallen in love with the land and put up the down payment with his own money. It became part of the yoga to make more money to make your land payments as well as your therapy payments to Chase. It was good to get away to the land where things were open and wild. The commune worked it out so that there was somebody up there at all times: in addition to the whole House going up every weekend, each person had to do a two-week stint up there totally alone (although they were in short-wave radio contact). They had tried to achieve a tribal community, a utopia within the brick walls of the loft. Once you were inside the tribal atmosphere of the House it was like being in a different world. From their penthouse vantage they could see the hollows and hills of San Francisco stretching off in all directions. But from their inner perspective, they could have been on another world.

KP and Walker got into the Stratford motel in Ashland, Oregon about 3:00 AM Saturday morning. They crashed for a few hours, got breakfast at 8:00, showered and were on the road by 9:00.

On the way to the trailer rental place, where Kong's new owner had left it for them, Walker wondered if the two pals were up to the adventure. Walker spent most of his days in front of a computer now, bathing his face in information. KP, a senior engineer for a telephony company, was not the KP of five years before—strong from chopping wood and hauling water—who had spent a year building a well rig, farming, and generally managing the land. But they were empowered by the sight of the great, mighty, and invincible KONG parked against the back fence. They felt any inadequacies in their physical ability would be made up for by Kong's technological power. They carefully rolled back the patched tarp and clear plastic sheet covering the driver compartment. There was no top, only a windshield sticking up out of the flat hood. KP, looking very much the connoisseur of eccentric automotive machinery, sat high in the open cockpit. With some judicious pumping on the gas peddle and working the choke in and out he got Kong fired up. “It has a 24 volt electrical system,” he said with pride. He backed it smartly around to where the rental agent dropped the hitch of a twenty foot trailer onto Kong’s chrome ball.

Coming back through Ashland, Kong drew lots of stares. KP and Walker didn’t dare take the beast on Interstate 5, so during a clear spell on that fall Saturday they motored the back roads, even crossing a covered bridge, in the topless vehicle with trailer in tow.

Walker remembered when, after Chase had died, and the community was going up to the highest place on the land for the lama to conduct a Tibetan funeral, how Kong had labored up the hill carrying almost half the commune up from the tents at the bottom of the land to Christmas Camp, near the top of the land. Then on that summer day, Kong went back down and picked up the lama and his retinue. The lama was a friend of Chase and recognized him as a religious genius, who had perhaps become holy. Kong came lumbering up the steep grade in low gear with about twenty House people on it. Some were sitting in the two bench seats that ran along the length of its bed over the rear wheels, their backs resting against the slats of Kong’s wooden sides. Some were sitting at their feet, huddled in the middle of the truck bed. Others were standing up, holding onto the stirrups of the canvas top that went over the driver compartment. Driving around this wild land in Kong was like being inside King Kong, the ultimate light assault vehicle.

The two men headed into the land on a fire road just off Interstate I-5, after crossing the border back into California. KP had driven Kong over this road many times before, but it had been five years. The road rises up off the interstate and goes through some high pasture lands, rising nearly 4000 feet onto a ridge. It passes through juniper and pine forest, and there are a couple of streams to cross before abruptly ending at the gate to the land. From there it was another half mile down to the tents. But it was in that first high pasture area, after just starting in, that they almost got stuck. It had been raining on and off for days and they quickly found themselves in deep mud. At first there were a few scary moments slip-sliding away in the mud because they hadn't switched Kong to 4-wheel drive, but the amazing Kong trucked right on through it anyway.

Over the roar of Kong's engine, Walker shouted, "Hey, Remember Natasha? Man. How she used to power those rent-a-cars through the mud. She was wild! Slipstreaming! Doing controlled drifts. Drove like some kind of back-woods dirt-track driver."

KP said, "Yeah. She was hell on wheels. You know, she came from around here, Susanville I think it was."

Walker remembered Natasha, her classical beautiful feeling face, like on a Greek statue, sometimes so elegant, sometimes flashing so much anger. The way she would look at you with her big sad eyes. He recalled her in lumberjack clothes powering the sedan through the ruts. Then he said, "Remember how good she looked in a teddy when we all went up to Harbin?"

"Yeah. Boy, she was beautiful. Like a Victoria's Secret model."

"Yeah, but man, her moodiness, and her hellish histrionics."

"Yeah. She had a great sadness. Suffered a lot of abuse. At the hands of her father."

They reached the old rendezvous point beneath Pilot Rock where the Pacific Crest Trail crosses the fire road leading to the land. Leaving Kong running, they got out.

KP, flush with empowerment from his driving acumen, seemed to be marveling at the satisfying crunch of his new boots on a dirt road. "Yeah. We used to start the walk in from here."

Walker observed, "Some peckerwood redneck has blasted the plaque marking the trail head with a shotgun. Pretty much cratering it."

The two men walked on a bit. "I remember Wyoming running up and jumping on Ursu," Walker said. He pictured Wyoming shrieking with excitement (which was unlike her because she was usually the cool, intellectual, analytical-therapist, Jewish hippie) in her tight jeans, leaping through the air and clasping Ursu around his waist with her legs, throwing her arms around his neck. And him staggering back and clasping her under the butt.

"Yeah, she was a wild one too," KP agreed. "She was always talking about the House moving to Wyoming. It was some kind of idea of wildness she had." After a pause he said, "You know she was the first woman I ever slept with. I was out of engineering school and still a virgin." He smiled with the memory. "Got seduced by an older, experienced women. Thank god! Of course I fell in love with her. And right away moved in to the House. It is amazing to think that I had lived a good part of my life in daily proximity to the first woman I ever made love with."

"Yep. We used to start the walk in from over there.

This is where I got my first view of Mount. Shasta," Walker said. "Man, I was enthralled. Can't see it today though."

KP said, "Looks like we'll get some more rain before this trip is through."

Walker remembered back to the time when he and KP started to in fact become friends. It was on that sad occasion on the walk out after the funeral ceremony when they had come to scatter Chase's ashes. The world seemed transcended, many were deep in thought as they walked the seven miles along the ridge back to the cars. The treks to and from the land were always used as a walking meditation anyway, the rocky terrain with snakes requiring one to put his full consciousness into each step. This time it was even sadder and more mystical with the lama having read the burial ceremony and intoning ancient anthems in an unknown tongue. The House knew what the ceremony was about because they had been reading the *Tibetan Book of the Dead* aloud, night after night for weeks in preparation for the funeral. The scriptures the Lama read were printed on long rectangular sheets of hand-made paper. As he finished a page, he would lift it carefully with both hands off the top of a stack, flip it over and place it neatly on a stack beside the other. These scriptures were wrapped in an ornate gold brocade cloth and kept in a jeweled wooden box. Each page had been printed from a wooden plate full of cuneiform runes carved by hand. The writing that was so current for the lama was as old as Beowolf, apparently discovered by Padmasambavda.

On the walk out Walker felt it necessary to lighten up the situation. He told a story he had read about a musical entomologist who taught crickets to play a theme from Mozart. A good conversation ensued with KP working out the technical problems of designing a microprocessor that would play Mozart. And Walker, tripping on the alliteration of insect instinct said, "Instinct is hard wired into the brain."

KP agreed: "It is not a programmable function like intelligence."

"Well what about finite automata?" Walker retorted. "I mean, it is a basic archetype of order like the circle. The insects are a representation of finite automata and what is our place in all this?" They explored the analogy of God as a divine ROM burner, writing the necessary intelligence into a being for it to perform the functions necessary for it to stay alive, and even prosper. They became good friends then. At first their friendship consisted of a friendly competition whenever they got together to see who could say the most outrageous stuff and make the other laugh. Over the years the charm, intellectual rigor, and enduring enthusiasm brought to these conversations developed into an attachment.

The two men climbed back on board Kong and headed on into the land. It was like being in one of those great early open automobiles, motoring the back roads of time. A little while further down the road, as they came around the side of a hill, Walker noticed two things at once: the stand of trees they were entering seemed to be all acting in concert as though turning to look down the draw; and the road they were on crossed a creek at the bottom of this grove. KP pulled over to the side. "Let's stop here a bit. This is the Wooded Glade. This is the prettiest spot on the whole trip." With satisfaction KP turned off the ignition and the quiet sun dappled sweetness of the shady grove impressed them with its presence of place. It was a most beautiful place—a stand of maple trees, an oddity in these parts—with the last of the fall color still on them. "These hardwood trees come together, near the water."

They stood there underneath the over-arching canopy. The place commanded a sense of awe and of mystic beauty. They walked among the spots of sunlight filtering through and dropping down to the forest floor in shafts. Here and there brilliant green moss grew on the side of dark boughs. The place seemed to hold moisture and good air to itself. They stood still in the wood and listened: first to the quiet of the place and eventually the soft hush of the wind filtering through the trees. An image came to Walker: The forest is the wind's cathedral.

Walker reached out his hand and stroked a patch of bright green moss growing on the side of a limb as though petting the fine fir of an animal. "Now this is . . . what I would call the preternatural sheen around all things," he said, in a strident way.

KP smiled and rolled his eyes. He liked a good turn of phrase. He liked to tease, to get a rise out of Walker. "Now, what do you mean by preternatural?"

And Walker liked to rise to the challenge: "Well, it is like you have phenomenon and you have noumenon." He puffed himself up like a pontificating philosopher. His voice began to curve in and out along the train of definitions and thought as he began speaking like an Indian with a British accent: "The phenomena is just a representation of the noumena. The preternatural sheen is when you get to see the phenomenal emerging from the noumenal. Becoming. It's kind of a quantum foam. You know, like in those beer commercials where they show a close up of the bubbles rising in the amber, then popping up off the surface in a shimmering fizz. It is like you can see back for a second, beneath the tissue, beneath the molecules, beneath, beneath, beneath, all the way back to the vacuum, which is in effect just a detente, an equilibrium between matter and antimatter. Well, in a similar way, when the being of something becoming pops over into observable existence, a kind of fulminating into being out of the phosphorescent cosmic foam, it sometimes presents a noumenal luminosity. And it is this light energy that is the preternatural sheen that surrounds all living beings."

"Oh yeah rr*rright.*" KP shook his head and chuckled. "I suppose this fits in with our romantic pictures of beauty in nature."

"That's the thing about the King Kong movie," Walker said. "His eyes. I mean they were just made out of glass, but it really made it, you know? Made them look all the more glassy and stony like looking into some kind of the amoral abyss of pure animal energy. That's what it was. Especially that scene where he has climbed up the building and is looking through the window at people, at a woman sleeping. Yeah, he picks her up. And when he sees that she's not the one, he drops her. And she falls into dark space."

After Wooded Glade they settled into the drive in. They did not stop until they reached the gate to the property. The post holding it up had been knocked over, and the gate had been pushed to the side of the road.

"People letting their cattle run on the land." KP said.

They continued along the winding road, skirting hills. The House had spent much time maintaining it. They stopped and turned off the engine at the top of the land.

"Let's walk around a bit," KP said.

They walked beneath the huge tree at the fork in the road, heading over to the orchard. As they walked passed the orchard, KP said, "I used to haul truckloads of fifty-gallon barrels of water in Kong from the pond down below. We would siphon it off into the reservoir barrels up here along the road above the orchard."

From there the water fed a drip irrigation system during the dry season. Theory was to plant an orchard on the north face in case of an early thaw so the fruit wouldn't bloom too early, and then have the whole crop lost by a return freeze. The high deer fence which had surrounded the orchard was bent down and twisted now. The reservoir barrels were rusted and full of rain water, and only two tough, stunted apple trees were still surviving.

Walker recalled crawling around among the young saplings and putting rich natural fertilizer in a ring around the base of each tree. It must have been comical to see this big gangly guy, following the little pagan tribes-women who were lithe and limber, tanned brown as Indians, moving among the tangles of the underbrush. As they maneuvered among the dense scrub bushes and trees, sometimes stooping, sometimes having to crawl on their hands and knees, sometimes making long steps in their bare feet to avoid the irrigation lines, Walker got flashes of shapely legs, bare thighs and brown buns, and even a bushy crack smiling back up at him. They made lots of noise: clanged things, chatted, and sang aloud, so no snakes would tolerate being in that orchard. He was new to the commune then and had not grown accustomed to hard work along side the commune women. Nor had he ever seen women who moved with such a relaxed, quiet sense of owning their physical person. On their land, they let the norms of dress fall away entirely and reveled in their birthday suits.

Walker and KP walked down the road past the orchard to a beautiful open vantage point. KP said, "This is where we were going to build a house. In sight of Mount Shasta, and Pilot Rock, and Chase's Peak." Walker stepped up and began balancing himself on a huge log. KP, arms extended, did likewise and balanced himself on another.

"We were going to build this huge barn," KP said. "We used Kong to pull logs out of the forest."

Nearby there were some huge beams milled on four sides. KP pointed to them and said, "This is a jig set up for splitting logs. We had this Alaskan saw mill and split a lot of our own logs. There's what's left of it."

Walker asked, "Do you remember that time we all had to pick up that huge tree? Chase had us pick up this giant log, remember? It must have been the whole House up there, and somehow—that was the heaviest thing I have ever lifted—we all managed to pick this big log up and get it up on our shoulders and like a giant centipede we walked in step—someone calling out left right, left right and we carried it up over the hill. It was like some kind of insane thing we were all GOING TO DO! We prided ourselves in being able to, I mean, we were like, you know—crazed monks on speed—*going to work together*, in this group endeavor just to prove that it could be done. No matter what. Onward soldiers of

Buddha! It was the heaviest thing I ever lifted."

"Ho ho, ha," KP chuckled. "Yeah, that was wild. I have often wondered about the hold that Chase had over us. He was into confronting everything, and giving us yogas to confront the ego at every turn. If a person had fear of heights he would be slowly walked over a high bridge in the company of trusted friends. If someone was afraid to drive on the freeway, by god they were going to drive on the freeway. A person who had a lot of disgust with their own nudity, would have to sit naked in group."

"Living in the House was one big yoga," Walker agreed. "Chase saw shame, guilt, and anxiety as illusions brought on by growing up in an environment of social injustice—the nuclear family. We had to confront that night after night by sleeping with someone else, in the same room as the person you slept with the night before! That sure did in jealousy, shame, guilt and anxiety. Or was supposed to."

KP said, "I bet if Chase had told us to start having children, to go forth and infest the countryside with superior beings, we would have done it. We wanted to get this large parcel of land, and create a self-sufficient place of peace, where all the electricity, all the water, all the food, all the education, all the necessary things are made or provided within."

"Yeah, it would have been good," said Walker. "Just think, no taxes, no utility bills, and you don't have to go to the government for anything. You have your own library, gardens, healers, bakery, create your own music and art—everything self-contained. That would be true community." Walker remembered his plans of having a few people living out on the land: engineers that designed and build electronics and had the manufacturing done elsewhere; designers living in hand built *palacios* with verandas built of native stone. There was a lot of it just lying around. He wanted the physical activity of working in stone to offset the mental activity. He had great dreams of a community of people living in organic architecture, spread out over the land and using photovoltaics and passive solar energy. He wanted to build up on Chase's Peak because it was in a line-of-site to the interstate, and they would have been able to transmit data back and forth using a small parabolic dish and a shortwave phone modem connecting them to Silicon Valley CAD houses and the rest of the world. Everywhere they looked, the land was imbued with their fantasies. It was like the promised land of Pure Land Buddhism for them. It was the place to support the lifestyle of Right Action and Right Speech and the other steps on the Eight-fold Path through sorrow. "Man, we had some dreams for this place."

"Do you recall the time we built a fire up among those chimney rocks up on Chase's Peak?" Walker asked. "It was like a natural flue, and we could burn a whole log upright and get this long fire. Me and you, wasn't it. Lucia wasn't along on that trip, was she? Oh yeah she was. We did that MDMA."

"Yea we did MDMA that time," recalled KP.

"God yes," Walker said. "I felt like Prometheus chained to a rock, just sweating and rushing."

"I was about to get really worried about you," KP grinned at his friend. "I thought we were going to have to tie you down there for a moment."

"Boy, I had the sweats something awful. I was trying to keep up with the rushes. But after a while it became quite nice up there, on those warm rocks."

Walker shook his head, recalling in dismay what hallucinogens put the body through. It was a full moon on that night too, he recalled. But it was a clear summer night. You could see little lights in the towns far below, and in the odd farmhouses scattered about on Shasta's massive prominence. Shasta had drawn a curl of cloud around itself like a shawl which seemed almost phosphorescent in the moonlight. The lights reminded him of a fantasy he had had as a child about a great mound in his backyard in which there was a honeycomb of caves tunneling through the earth, caves that did not obey the normal laws of space and time, but which were shortcuts going across great distance and emptied out into other worlds.

But on that night on the land they could see the vast cross section of the Milky Way, spread out across the night sky. The earth was looking back into the center of our galaxy but it looked like seeds being thrown by the sower of stars, moving out in a great arch to scatter into fields of infinite darkness. He had been touched by the universe that night. He said, "That was one of the few times in my life when I saw extraterrestrial things. You were there. You saw it too, didn't you?"

"Yes, I have to admit I did," agreed KP.

"There WERE these lights," Walker recalled. . . ."We could have been looking down the afterburner of jets, but there was no sound of being buzzed and the lights moved so fast. But they lit up the place like klieg lights! Remember that ?"

"Yeah, I . . . do," said KP, suspicious of his own admission.

"It was like those big lights you see coming from a

helicopter," said Walker, "except there was no sound. No sound at all. I felt like calling after the lights, saying: 'We're down here, come and get us. Take us with you. We'll go with you anywhere.'

"I mean I like to freak you know," Walker continued, "but that's just fiction. And you, you're as hard-headed, as orthodox, a British empiricist as they come. I have never been able to get a satisfactory explanation for myself on that one. Have you?"

"Probably gravitational anomalies," KP mumbled like some cornered scientist indicating he didn't quite believe that explanation either.

"Could be." Walker reasoned, "It was like our fire was communicating with Mount Shasta. . . . Mount Shasta holds weather to itself, and maybe, spirits as well. After all it is a holy place. The lama had come and done the burial ritual here. It has been consecrated by a real lama."

Walker thought more about the ritual of Chase's funeral. It was about the passing of a great soul into the beyond, just like the sun they watched setting from up on that peak, a warm barren place. And all the people of the House, picking up pinches of ashes and shards of bone, walking in slow single file, warily, to the edge of the cliff, and dropping them over the abyss. How the human ashes drifting down, in the waning sunlight of the day shifting over to dusk glistened, almost like diamond dust, as they fell over the edge and lofted out on the updrafts, on their way back to the earth.

He had stood on the roots of a dead tree at the edge of the cliff then, looking at the valley down below and watched the dust ashes sparkle in the setting sunlight as they fell, floating on his sense of the whole world body, brain, community, work, love, life—the world of cycles, the metabolism cycle, the Krebs cycle.

It was after the Tibetan funeral and the scattering of ashes into the landscape that Walker had had a vision of a great glass skull floating in the clouds over the central valley. It was smiling a grateful-dead smile, a blue light fading from the base of the spine. The skull was crystal so that light refracted through it, the eyes never blinked, never, not once. They saw all being passing through, saw reality as a shimmering mirage moving across a landscape in spring-time.

Walker and KP got back into Kong and continued down the road from the orchard at Christmas Camp for another steep half mile, over some narrow spots, past the barn site to the tents. This was the camp proper. Two huge wall tents had been butted together end on end to make one long tent. The front door gave out onto the parking area. Walker didn't remember the large cleared porch area in front of the tent. Then he realized one of the tents was gone. It had been taken out by a previous cleanup crew. The plywood roof which had covered it was still attached to the other tent and was now fallen down into the tamped earth floor.

The tents had once looked like an encampment of Gypsies; now it looked like an encampment of refugees. The A-frame skeleton showed through the sagging olive drab. Over time, gaffer's tape had been applied everywhere in vain hopes of holding back the tears. Though one tent was gone, the floors were still level and the down-slope retaining wall of stone was still true.

The tent was nestled in the crook of a gentle slope, and the back door was by a stream that flowed down to the pond at the bottom of the land. The out-of-the-house was an open two-seater with a little corrugated plastic roof over it. It was situated just a few yards from the back door tent. KP stared at the tent a moment before picking up a long stick and approaching through the back door. He stooped and walked into the tent, gingerly poking the stick ahead of himself for snakes and critters. Inside he moved past the flat sand fire-box platform upon which the wood stove had been situated. "I used to worry about the Coleman lamps, with their white-hot mantles catching a tent on fire."

Over against the wall, the library had fallen down, and books about psychology, Carlos Casteneda, midwifery, living in the woods, were spilled out on the floor. When they came back outside, they were feeling discouraged. KP looked up toward the barn site beside the tent and the road out and said, "I just feel like splitting." They looked at the sad frayed canvas hung up on poles covering the structure. KP looked down the road which went over a little hill and ended at the bottom of the land were the pond was. They were greatly saddened, remembering the land in its heyday when the tents were inhabited by lively young adventurous communards, attractive people who looked like they would be at home in a pre-Raphelite jousting camp. They used to have colored prayer socks on poles blowing in the wind, the wind carrying these prayers like whispers of the earth up to the hills, on up to the mountains and beyond out into space. On the hot central valley summer days when you could see the heat rising in shifting plumes of air, they would roll up the sides of the tent and have these big group pow wows, talking about all the things the tribes-people needed to talk about. It was like a meeting of people in medieval times. Jousters in the service of their liege, jousting—with neurosis. Walker said, "It is really sad what this place has come down to."

KP said, "Let's get our gear set up, start a fire then go down to the pond."

After putting a kettle of water on the edge of the low fire, they pitched their little two-man tent. KP said, "Let's walk down to the pond while there is still some light and see if the goldfish are still there." After they had walked a bit KP told the story of how he had gone to a mall and bought up *all* the gold fish this pet store had for sale. He carefully transported them up to the land in order to set them free in the pond, so they could flow back into nature. "Man, it made me feel like a monk! I want to see if they survived."

They walked the quarter mile down to the pond. At the lowest point on the land, where the road went across the creek, were the remnants of the well rig. It was another marvel of engineering to trap water. They had built a tripod by lashing together three huge telephone poles into a point. This, sitting on a triangular base of railroad ties, formed a tetrahedron—the most stable of all structures. It looked like a medieval catapult. KP, who was an engineer in real life (as were several of the men in the House) had checked out books on the catapult and learned all about timbers and medieval engineering and become an expert in knots. The well drilling project made him feel like a hero in the House. He loved going back in time to an age of mechanical engineering before the age of electricity. They used the gas generator to pound pipe sleeves into the earth. The people of the House were into self-sufficiency to the point of arrogance. They tried to do everything for themselves; they hated dependency in any form. And now strewn about the structure was steel casing, chain, iron pry bars, and lots of hardware and steel cable. But the grass had grown over it, and hidden much of it from view.

From there the road led up a little hill before dropping down to the man-made pond. This hill rose up and opened out in the middle of their valley. The early rising moon could be seen coming up over the rim of the ridge. Reaching the top of the hill, they paused a moment to breathe. Walker felt strange. It was as if he were a stranger on this land, as if they had never been there. Even when he had been up here by himself for extended periods of time, it didn't feel this desolate. Now it felt so alone and desolate out there, it was as if no one had ever been there. The land was reclaiming itself. It was a living thing moving so slowly you could only catch it out of the corner of your eye, and then you had to turn around real fast. It was as if he were an alien returned from strange worlds to his own native planet. It had been his home. For a brief time he was in a family. After a brief time of this tribe treading softly on the land—and not so softly on it—the land had taken back this sense of home. It was gone.

There was a little patch of woods on top of the hill which Walker approached with trepidation. It was here that he had seen the vision of Dahlia as the Woman in the Woods. It embarrassed him now—the memory, it was like a picture on a holy card, or some blue saturated Hindu depiction of Krishna. Blue-fringed to the sky filtering through the leaves—the memory. Dahlia steps into the clearing out of the forest looking like a wood nymph cradling a baby fawnlette in her arms! She had actually managed to pick up this stray baby deer. This image was so enshrined in Walker's memory that he had to smile. The leaves around her image formed a lacy fanlight, a halo of bioenergy as she emerged from the forest. A fawn had been abandoned by its mother and Dahlia was rescuing it. Heavenly god, what a vision of loveliness. I sure had it bad for that girl. But now he was both chagrined and delighted that he could escape the hold her image had on him by thinking of how some of the others in the House got on her case saying, "The mother had just moved away and now here was this meddling white woman carrying off her baby."

KP and Walker looked up at a V-formation of honking geese flying south. They stood at the edge of the pond looking at the water for a good long while. KP moved in closer. "Look!" he said. "I saw a goldfish. And look. There's another. Can you see it?" Walker strained his eyes but couldn't see any fish. Then, moving closer to the water, he saw one. "Yes. I see one."

By now KP had walked hurriedly around to the deep end at the sump wall. There he saw a whole school of fish basking in the afternoon sun at the end of the day. "The pond is teaming with goldfish!" he yelled excitedly. A little later they were sitting up on the bank overlooking the pond shimmering in the setting sun. KP looked upstream. "Water," he sighed. "It is all about trying to preserve a little water, trying to keep it from escaping."

Walker thought about the golden fish in the sump. They had achieved some kind of ecological homeostasis, the amount of foliage disbursing the oxygen in the water for the fish was enough to trap food to keep the school thriving. They would continue to thrive.

KP said, "I'm so glad there are fish still in the pond. At least it proves that there is something here that outlasted us."

Back at the campsite they pooled their food. After dinner they stoked up the fire and hunkered down around it, each sitting on one of the log benches that had been laid out in a square around the circle of the fire pit. The fire pit was under a giant Douglas fir whose trunk shot up two stories before sprouting any branches. It was the perfect tree to be around a fire underneath, to watch the smoke rise up into its boughs, and waft on up into the stars. The fire's fast shape-shifting yet slow-moving etiology engaged them. Sleepy, dreamy, warm, comforting camp fire in the moist night. If you listen to it, crackling and popping, it is like some great, clumsy, slow-moving being stumbling in the dark woods on the periphery of the fire. It devours dead wood. It pulls the air in around itself like the darkness is some slow moving kind of other-dimensional gaseous entity being inhaled.

"Were you there when the House hired those couples therapists to come in and help?" KP asked.

"Oh, yeah."

"That's right. A lot of people weren't there during the final break-up. They were smart."

"Dhalia had already split, but I was in another group."

"I wish I had split. It was pretty bad. The House was in trouble. All the couples were separating. The group marriage was dissolving. We were coming apart at the seams! We had tried various things, meditation, chanting, but a sangha without its spiritual leader is a sad thing indeed. We were so desperate that we decided to try even traditional counseling, which we had always held beneath contempt before.

"It was wild," continued KP. "Wasn't it? Here we had this steely-eyed young therapist in a blue serge suit—wearing wingtips no less, coming to the House. And his wife. They were a couple that did couples therapy. Her name was something like Jennifer Flowers, and his was Jason for god's sake. I kid you not. And they lived in Marin! We were always so damn cocky. We started psychoanalyzing *them*, trying to find out about their relationships. They had met at the university and got married young.

"We tried to tell them about dependency."

"Oh, dependency." Walker scoffed. "I got so tired of hearing that word all the time. It was like, if you started getting too close to one of the women, they started telling you, 'You're becoming too *dependent*.'" Walker said this last word with a valley-girl whine. "Come to think of it, my last girl friend said that to me too. Is it a California thing?"

"Yeah I know, the men used that term on the women too," said KP. "It was like, in the House, 'Evil, thy name is dependency.'" He made the sign of the cross with his fore fingers, holding it in front of himself while hissing through bared teeth, as if he were trying to ward off a vampire coming at him from the darkness beyond the fire.

"We told them about how we experimented with LSD, Tibetan mysticism, primal scream therapy, neo-Reichian body bioenergetics, Zen and every other radical psychology you could think of from the sixties,"

KP said. "We told them about how Chase started sleeping with his patients. How he had designed a group therapy that went beyond traditional analysis, and did what group therapy was supposed to do: let people see what it is like to put projections on other people in group, and for people in group to learn how to deal with these projections. In group, people are supposed to learn how to become therapist for each other. It was supposed to take the responsibility away from the therapist having to shoulder all the burden of these projections in a practice, so that he could grow too. So everybody could grow."

Walker said, "It was s'posed to be non-hierarchical."

"That's right," KP said. He stared at the fire for a long moment. The flames looked like tiny enraged workmen throwing up their arms in a frenzied effort of coherent destruction. Dancing phantoms, whose feet were rooted, seemed the other side of shadows, flickered light then morphed into shrouds. He looked over at Walker and smiled. "I wonder what those two shrinks thought when they first came to see Big Group assembled?"

Walker pictured the two innocent therapists dropped into the center of the circle of Big Group. The whole commune, the tribe, the group marriage, the sangha, all around in a circle, quietly looking back at them with big innocent childlike eyes. Walker exclaimed in mock horror: "A *menage a quarante*! Right in the heart of the city!"

KP chuckled. "Boy, we must have been a shock for them." He shook his head in dismay. "There they were—suddenly confronting the beast itself."

"They must have seen it arising out of the center of

Big Group!" Walker said with a chortle. He laughed and shook his head. He reached out and poked the fire with a stick. He thought about tribes, people in the ancient circle around the fire. These plucky, innocent therapists coming to do couples therapy on a menage was like an anthropologist stumbling in on a tribe that had an entirely different belief structure, a separate consensus reality, worshipping this giant Being, the Group Mind, emerging from the center of the ring. A group mind, which had gone off en-masse in search of its feelings, its beauty, its bliss, its birthright. And it was having one gigantic identity crisis, like some teenager who had been caught having sex.

"You had this web of relationships," said KP, "that you had to maintain with so many people. The fact that you knew that the next night you would be sleeping with somebody else forced you to be on good terms with them if you could. This web of relationships is the group mind."

"And these were hot intense sexual relationships," Walker added, "in which you were admonished by the other people in the web to go as deeply as possible."

"We told them about the group mind," KP said. "That the group mind that the House had discovered was the same group mind that the sanghas had recognized for over a thousand years. We tried to tell them that we were part of a lineage, that we were descendants in a lineage of lama and sangha going back thousands of years to tantric cults living a utopian existence on the shores of India.

"We told them we knew these utopian communes were later overrun by the Roman empire. That the people who lived in them were so blissed-out and had been peaceful for so long they forgot hostility and were easily overrun. But in the modern protected city of America you don't need to worry about being overrun. Supposedly. You could be rational about designing your life style. Utopian communes based upon group marriage could be established again. All you need to do is keep a low profile."

"Unlike Rajaneesh," Walker added.

"Yea, *those* guys," sniffed KP. "In their lavender cotton sweats—uniforms. They were totally into confrontation and image.

"We told them that the group mind of the House had achieved a certain critical mass, which could overthrow the tyranny of the culture at large and come to a consensus reality. We told them the House was a presence, it was like a minor god—that got into your consciousness, did battle with the forces of oppression there—your parents. We told them, 'The enemy has an outpost inside your own head.'"

KP continued, "But they told us, that we had substituted the group mind with its own watchfulness for that watchfulness of the parents or super-ego. And that this watchfulness, (things were 'owned and reported in groups' kind of like the Catholic confessional) was getting mixed up with our own paranoia generated by the ego in defense to being confronted all the time.

"I've talked to some of the women since then," KP said. "They have told me they felt terribly vulnerable."

"The women felt very vulnerable," answered Walker. "Sure. Who wouldn't feel vulnerable. Having to sleep right next to somebody—your competition—night after night. And we didn't kill each other. It proves it can be done."

"Made it easy to have sex without orgasm," said KP.

"Right." said Walker. "If you didn't get off one night, chances are you would the next, or the next. It just kind of made you hornier and hornier night after night until the next night. Kind of like male nymphomaniacs."

"Yeah, right." KP chuckled. "After days and days of no orgasm in sex, you were ready to explode."

"Made you want to fuck like crazed weasels," Walker added. KP laughed.

"But then next night in group," continued Walker, "the woman would get on your case, challenge you about it, like 'Your ego wanted to stop the feelings.' We were kind of ridiculous, the guys having to own up in group: 'Sorry, I came.'"

Walker added with a satisfied smile: "'And did I ever.'"

"Yeah, that's for sure," said KP. "Theoretically you got this sexual glow from maintaining a sexual energy, it was your passion glowing. We couldn't have done it except we were in therapy all the time. It was like trying to convert the fires of your ego, which was being assaulted from all corners—that's what the House did, it confronted the ego at every turn so that you saw how your construct of the world was made of straw and you watched it burn up in the rage at having your constructs taken away and you were supposed to convert that rage into a passion, into a love until it was a fire at the center of the psyche, and even though the ego was constantly resisting and sometimes positively kicking and screaming, you were able to see that as the fuel of the fire and put your constructs aside and see the world for what it actually is—and turn that heat from constant confrontation into an intimate passion for the people in your group. We told those shrinks we see it as bioenergy—bioenergy out penetrating and percolating and permeating this whole world. And big group inventing and discovering and experimenting with these various yogas to handle it."

Walker agreed. "You must be in therapy all the time, to be able to handle that many relationships. And you need to constantly be working on these relationships. It was like two fires. The fire of the ego resisting, and the glow of passion that you carried to bed night after night."

"Anyway," KP sighed, "they talked to us about commitment. They said if we were going to stay together we would have to renew our *commitment.* It was all about commitment. So that became the big word on everybody's lips for the last few months of the House. Commitment."

Walker sighed and smiled in resignation. "But I guess after years in group therapy people were *burning* to get out."

"Well," said KP, "we had the experience of a lifetime, got a deep understanding of psychology and group therapy that we can take out into life. Almost half of the people from the house went on to become therapists or teachers of one sort or another."

"Yeah, and a lot of couples ended up together," Walker said.

"Yeah, that's true. And a lot of good friends. What more could you ask for."

After a while Walker said, "Why don't we just carry a bit of this fire over to the tents and torch them up? Let the House go out in a blaze of glory."

KP look at him incredulously, and wondered if he was serious.

"Set the whole tent on fire?" he asked.

"Set the whole tent on fire!" Walker answered. "With all this rain and wet weather it would probably be safe."

KP saw that he was serious. "Nooo. All that plastic? It would stink something awful You'd get clouds of toxic smoke."

Walker turned his face toward the hills to the west, and gazed at the bruised grey rainstorm clouds moving fast in front of the full moon. "Well, with all this rain and wet weather it would probably be just fine. The grass is wet, nothing is going to catch fire. There is a lot of good dry wood under the tarp. Lets do it. Burn down the House."

KP looked mischievous for a moment. He caught the allusion and sang the phrase from the Talking Heads song: "'Burning down the House'. I like that. But, we better not."

A soft misty rain enveloped the camp during the night. It was a struggle the next morning, moving around in the small two-man tent, trying to put boots on without getting socks wet with some condensation on the tent walls getting into their clothes. Walker got the fire started, and made some strong coffee in a little aluminum two-cup coffee-maker he liked to use on camping trips. KP kept on going over and over the most efficient way to use the machinery while stirring honey out of what looked like a toothpaste tube into his tea. "We could load up the fifty-gallon drums here at camp, to give more height to Kong's sides, then start down at the bottom of the land. That way when we pick up all the stuff down there, we would see a much bigger improvement then we would see up here."

So they put two rows of empty fifty-gallon oil drums onto Kong's bed and the bed of the trailer and lumbered off down the narrow road to the bottom of the land. They spent the whole morning picking up the hundreds of white pickle buckets that had been baked brittle by the sun and stacking them inside each other on Kong. And the rest of the day dismantling the well, taking down and rolling up fence. The truck and trailer gradually were strategically piled high—stacks of buckets, hot water heater, old tire, rolled up fence wire. KP stood in his mud-caked boots in the rain with a faint resentment at having had the weekend taken away from him. He smiled with accomplishment though, at having the trailer so well loaded. Walker got under the shelter of the tool shed roof, stamping on one foot then shifting to the other foot for warmth. He looked at Kong. The buckets within containers within drums looked like some kind of a strange Rube Goldberg contraption of cylinders within cylinders . . . stacked into telescoping, towering tubes almost like different size pipes of a great moving pipe-organ. He said, "It looks like something out of The Cat In the Hat Comes Back." Indeed, it was a fugal contrapunction of crates and boxes, sticks and poles, that had once been part of something, to jostle and bounce against the big cylindrical water heater and sheets of metal to clang and shiver in place. It would make the most ungodly aleatory composition above the rumble of the engine and the road. "It's gonna be a major cacophony when we go—Shake, Rattle and Death—across the landscape," he said.

They appraised the situation. KP said, "The prospect of trying to cook a dinner out at the fire pit in the rain does not interest me."

Walker said, "Man, we've done all we can here. I say we go back in with the load we have. We were only half-way planning to make *two* dump runs anyway and you know how we always take on projects bigger than we usually can do."

"There are only a couple hours of light left," said KP, "and if we are to have the slightest chance of making it back to Ashland before dark we would have to split immediately."

"Yes! Immediately we must stop trying to wedge the last thing onto the truck, strike camp, load up our things and skedaddle on out of here!"

"Let's go for it."

In a mad dash, they quickly gathered up their camping gear, and wedged it behind the seat. Walker had the tent on the floor under his feet and was holding on to the ice chest situated on the seat between them. They headed out.

Right away, powering out of the place, where the lowland mud of the valley meets the sandy loam of the hill, they started to slide. They started to slide over a cliff, down into an arroyo. Kong seemed to be running with a mind of its own, off the edge of the road. KP turned the wheel away from the slide, his eyes buggin' as Kong just kept sliding toward the cliff. Going over the edge meant more than falling a long way, with all this heavy metal around them. It would be a horrible place to crawl out of with a broken leg. KP looked out over the edge of the road where Kong had started to take a nose dive. Panicked and enraged—white in the face—

he screamed, "Get this ice-chest offa of me!"

Walker suddenly shook himself to get ready for Kong to take a fall, go tumbling down the hill, and the trailer full of metal oil drums and cans and the hot water heater come crashing down around him. He practically had the ice chest on top of him and was sandwiched between the door and their camping gear. Would it be better for him to jump and try to avoid the trailer?

Annoyed, KP looked across to the other side of the truck where Walker had braced himself rigid. Walker was looking straight ahead, clutching the ice chest, trying to keep it away from impeding the driver.

It was indisputably pouring, when KP finally got Kong stopped with its two left tires just an inch away from rolling them over the edge into oblivion.

"Eeeeeeyowwww!" Walker moaned. "Just stop for a moment."

KP gripped the wheel, his knuckles white as he looked over at Walker.

"OK," he said, as he exhaled a sigh of relief.

"Now what about letting it just roll back slow," Walker said. "Let it roll straight back."

"OK."

"That's right, the trailer is gonna pull us back."

"It's hard as hell to steer this thing in reverse."

"Just let the ruts and the weight pull us back."

"OK."

Slowly, Kong rolled back finding its own way in the deep mud ruts. Walker knew that the best attack would be to reverse the backward momentum and blast on out of there without waiting for Kong to come all the way to a stop, where they would get further stuck trying to break the inertia again.

"OK, man. Gun it. Let's get out of here."

KP smiled as he held onto the fishtailing Kong as it pulled slightly forward.

Walker felt that KP needed a little extra prodding to especially pour it on so they didn't get stuck again.

"Mad Dog Phelan! Mash on the foot-feed!" he yelled at KP with a taunting smile. "Put your foot to the floor!"

KP stomped on it. "Don't call me Mad Dog," he said, hurt. Suddenly their momentum changed direction and they were pulling ahead onto the road.

"It worked!" shouted Walker. To assuage KP's bruised ego, Walker gave himself an even worse appellation. He said, "Mad Dog and Mud Dog save their own hides!"

KP looked over at Walker. He laughed. "You do look like hell up a tree."

Walker busted out laughing when he realized how freaked-out and mud-spattered he must look. "I feel like a mud-rat looking over a picket fence at white people."

They slapped high-five. To warm themselves up and take their minds off the freezing ride in the rain, Walker started singing in a loud, out-of-key voice with a British accent. "What can you do with a Drunken Sailor, Ear lie in the mourn in." KP joined in and they kept up the song for a while, obliterating the chill to the accompaniment of bang, rattle and clang of Kong's jostling load.

The rain started again and of course Kong's wipers continued in their nonworking state of torpor, which was just as well as there was no roof anyway. The great light assault vehicle hauled their frozen sorrowful asses up and down the hills, through the land, past Christmas Camp, past the Wooded Glade, and finally down the road, to a warm motel with hot showers. They parked the loaded Kong across the street in the closed Safeway parking lot. It was after closing hours; the dump run would be tomorrow. With the driver's compartment underneath the skin of a tarp, and the precariously perched stacks of cylinders looking like powerful exhaust pipes, what had once almost been their death-mobile looked like some kind of strange crawling Offenhouser junk monster escaped from Oil Can Alley, there with ropes hanging off it, quietly hobbled in the rain.

The next day (tired, weary, happy to be alive and mud free), the two men enjoyed hurling great heaps of metal off the truck and trailer, after KP did some elegant maneuvering at the edge of the landfill. They didn't say much. After returning the trailer, Walker followed in the Saab as KP drove Kong through some pretty farmland back to the owner's Tudor spread. Then they headed home down I-5 toward San Francisco in the Saab. As they drove past Mount Shasta on the interstate, Walker could hear the wheels of his own mind turning: Enough of this life-style experimentation. I have prepared myself for this. It is time to put myself in the picture. I will ask the lovely Sam to marry me. Really investigate commitment and dependency. It would all be new to me.

Once decided, Walker slipped into that onrushing free fall you get, when your life gets a gravitation pull from destiny. It is kind of giddy, like sailing of the edge of a cliff and falling from the 10,000 foot level. And the fall had just begun. Kevin would be his best man.

The Prowess of Kong

Modeling Marriageability

Having decided he was ready for the commitment of marriage, Walker set out to make himself what the women his age called marriageable. He did not have a lot of experience with dating. He had gone through years and years of psychotherapy, and had spent a small fortune on shrinks. He tended to use them as friends during long periods of loneliness. He had learned, at least, some of the language of intimacy. He let the preliminary courtship proceedings intensify. He started introducing Sam to his more successful friends—not the dope dealers and boulevardiers on SSI. There were some sophisticated dinners, in which people ordered Perrier water and sopped up oil in a side plate like Europeans.

Walker's model of a bachelor getting married late in life was his beloved maternal uncle, Roddy MacDougall. He was one of a big family of Scots who lived on a farm in Ontario and got married late in life. You guessed it, at forty-three. If you asked him, Walker would say, "He was perhaps the finest man I have ever known. Somehow acting the way my uncle does, helps me get in touch with the sense of goodness a man is capable of. He had a kind of humility and stalwart concern and attention. It is a magnanimous feeling."

Walker's emulation of his uncle was more unconscious than conscious. For, after all, it is a law of kinship anthropology, that if a boy does not hold up his father as an image of ideal manhood, he will hold up his maternal uncle. It is a law of animus / anima of archetypal psychology too. This also hooked into the great problem of the compensating narcissist—child of a household in alcoholic turmoil and denial—which was not knowing how to be. (The problem is actually deeper, and inherent in the subterfuge of *knowing* how to be.) But Walker didn't even know that then. Just thinking of Uncle Roddy made Walker smile. And the relief from the anxiety of not knowing how to be was like happiness, spreading. What is Roddy's secret? Love! A kindly agape, a generous hopeful enthusiasm. Where did he get that. And can I get some?

Sam too, sought to make herself a marriageable woman. She confided in her old friend Joan. The two women had become friends around being hippie jewelry artisans in the 70's. Over the years they had become quite different. Sam ended up working in a steady government job and now was in her own condo and had her own business. While Joan, ever the soulful knockabout, had fallen into somewhat of a downward spiral lately, drinking and smoking and doing a lot of drugs. However Joan is the married one—living in the Mission—with her construction worker husband and their child, a daughter. Since Sam hadn't had a relationship in years, she quite respected Joan's down-to-earth opinions about relationships. The two women met over a plastic table cloth in a booth in a cheesy downtown Chinese restaurant. Joan had ordered a pitcher of beer. Sam felt one of the petals of the peonies is a vase on the table to see if it was real; it was.

Sam: You know in my life I have had only about two long-term relationships, one in high school with John and one with Bill in my late teens, until age twenty-four. I was living with him and teaching school when you and I met.

Joan: But a couple of years ago you were goin' out with Raphael. What about Raphael?

Sam: Oh, god. That wasn't long term. And it ended bitterly and I never speak about it.

Sam looked at her friend for sympathy and saw a rueful, teasing confirmation there.

Joan, already a bit into her cups, sang a rock lyric, ". . . Just another notch on my guitar. . ."

Sam raised her eyes towards heaven in exasperation and said, "I'm just not the dating type."

Joan: You're not the dating type?

Sam: No, I'm not. People have told me as much. No, they think I'm the marrying type. I'm supposed to be the marrying type. At least that's what people have told me.

Joan: Who told you that?

Sam: Well the first time I heard it was in high school. And other guys have told me that I'm too bossy.

Joan: Well we *know* that.

Sam gave Joan an arch look. She blurted out the

issue for which she had called this meeting: "Now I'm in a relationship. With Walker. And I think it is going to go somewhere. And I really want it to happen."

"ALL RIGHT!" Joan exclaimed, looking genuinely delighted.

Sam: I don't want to blow it.

Joan shrugged and said, "Well you know, it's your own fault that people think you are not the dating type."

Sam: It is not!

Joan looked sympathetic and confided in a semi-humorous, semi-sincere way, "Guys are afraid of you."

"Afraid of me?" Sam drew back in mock denial and acted hurt. "Why?"

Joan: What have they told you? They've told you that you're too bossy. Guys know you're not the sort of girl to mess around with. You are to be taken seriously. You aren't going to put up with a lot of crap so if they aren't at the point to commit, then they don't even bother.

Sam felt dismayed. She had pretty much given up on ever finding a man equal to her intellectual passions and resigned herself to living alone in her condo. Especially since this dreadful AIDS thing was ravaging the population and people were just starting to understand it. She didn't have a boyfriend, hadn't gone out in years, and she wanted one. Instead she had gotten very active in her church, singing in the choir and going on various singles encounters. And picnics. She loved singing in the choir, and they were all such good friends, enjoying the excellent heartfelt songs the Jesuits wrote with the utmost surety in their faith. (Well. . . she *was* in some kind of competition with the *other* soprano diva in the group).

Sam said, “I had pretty much resigned myself to life of living alone in the condo. Then along comes this *guy*—walks right into my book—store and now we’re going out. And now my roommate, Jennifer, is moving out and Walker is kind of talking about living together.”

Joan: Hmmmm.

Sam: I haven’t had a boyfriend in so long. And you KNOW I wanted one. It’s kind of like I’m still living at home with my parents, even though I’ve got my own place. When does a women get to be her own person?

Joan: Not until you get married. Until then you’re just a daughter.

Sam: Well. I need some better escape plan to get out of my mother’s house. One featuring potential snugglebunnies.

The two women smiled. Joan gave Sam a seductive, lascivious wink.

Joan: But who said you weren’t the dating type anyway?

Sam: It’s happened a couple of times. When I was going to school at the Marynol Sisters Academy on 19th Avenue and we used to go out with the boys from across the way at St. Ignatius; I used to hang out with the geeks and one of them said I was—and I quote: not the type you date, but the marrying type, end-quote.

Joan: The ‘marrying type’. ’Sup wit dat, anyhow?

Sam: It is like some kind curse laid on you. When I was a sophomore, my beau was a junior, John; very thin, wore glasses and had a goofy smile. A silly disposition. A really sweet guy. A nerd. The guys he hung out with were all intellectual-types into sci-fi and chess and science labs and math. . . you know, geeks. Don’t get me wrong—we all were, myself included. For some reason they adopted *me*. Somehow, I was the type of geek who had permed hair, big earrings and a penchant for mini-skirts. We were all so innocent, good catholic kids, shocked by the idea of even the slightest sexual innuendoes. Anyway John turned out to be gay! It broke my heart. He came out in the Summer of Love! I began to feel like I was cursed. We went to an all-girls, Catholic high school—we had to take what we could get!

Then, from the time I was nineteen until twenty-four, I was with Bill. He was a musician, and all they wanted to do was play. We met Bob and Priscilla, and started hanging around with that crowd.

Joan: Yeah, I didn't see too much of you those years.

Sam: We were rock-and-roll royalty wanna-be's. I really dressed the part, had all those groovy hippie mod clothes and we hung out at clubs. Since my boy friend was a musician.

Joan: But who else told you you were of the marrying kind?

Sam: Well, then, if that wasn't bad enough, I got pronounced-on by one of the Nuns.

Joan: Really!

Sam: It was like I went to some kind of career analysis test and they came up with the label 'Homemaker'! It was like this nun was essentially saying, "I have the results right here, ma'am."

"Ma'am? I'm only sixteen."

"Ah, but you are the Marrying Type! Your scores are high in cooking, washing, cleaning with great loathing and abhorrence for dirt and disease. And you're are obsessively punctual. AND fidelity is a mark of honor with you."

Thank YOU, Mother Superior!

Joan: Well what the heck do they know anyhow. They're nuns. Married to Jesus. Get *none.*

Sam: I mean, Leave-it-to-Beaver's mother, I'm not!

But I heard it again in college. When I was with Bill, who was like John except with a ponytail. Just because I was the kind of girl who doesn't sleep around, cares genuinely for her loved ones and is faithful in her affections I get labeled as 'the marrying type.' I was supposed to go to Law School. Get into politics. But my parents cut me off, when I went to a protest. Anyway now I'm older and wiser and no longer filling into tight jeans the way I used to . . .

Joan: Me neither. Who can? Look at me!

Sam: And my wild dating days are over—as if I ever had any wild dating days. I have got to make some kind of an escape plan or I'm going to end up alone with my parents!

Joan shook herself in recognition. She said, "Oooh, Ick! Did I tell you that my *mother* got arrested? Yeah, it was in the local drugstore in San Rafael. She refuses to pay the price for premium brands and refuses to use generics."

Sam: God, that's awful. What did you do.

Joan: I had to go down to the jail house and bail out my own mother!

Sam: I don't know what I'm going to do when I have to have Walker meet *my* parents. I'd hate to have him meet my *mother*. My mother is such a bitch. I mean I know people think *I'm* a bitch but I'm NOT. A bitch is a woman who is nasty for no reason. We all act bitchy, at times.

Joan: Even guys. Seems guys are always in some

kind of pissing contest.

Sam: Yeah.

Joan: But really, a guy fears he will get the snot knocked out of him, whereas women think they can get away with it.

Sam: I used to just cringe whenever I had to go with her into a Post Office with her. She'd get so angry and impatient in line. She'd always look like she was about to break something. She'd heave these big, long, exasperated sighs, muttering "Oh, *god*, they are completely understaffed here!" She would say this just loud enough for everyone around her to hear and instantly begin to hate her. And she is so cheap!

Joan: Yeah, that generation came through the Depression and they never forgot it.

Sam: Last Mother's Day I got her a Mother's Day card and the first thing she does is turn the card over to check the price on it—BEFORE reading it.

The two women parted because Sam had to get a streetcar back to the office.

Walker started the marriage question going when the two went on a hike up to the West Point Inn on Mount Tamilpais in Marin. Sam had worn the cutest little pair of short-shorts in the world, even though it was November. Her legs gave Walker the wolf-eyes. He got her to snuggle up with him in a chaise lounge, keeping her warm, and in the moment, and coming to know her "marrying type qualities," he said, "I'd really like to have a child with you."

That's what did it.

Since it wasn't THE question, she didn't have to answer right away but that really got the machinery started. She had just heard the wake up alarm of her biological clock and it was ticking louder. A few days after that when she brought it up, and said, "This means we will have to get married," he agreed.

Sam was big on church and wanted a Catholic wedding. They bought rings and put them on her credit card. He didn't have a credit card, liked to pay as he goes. She got a beautiful ring. It was a wide band with a twist in the gold, and in the twist there were mounted three diamonds. He got fitted out with a simple band. They started going to the pre-Cana convention in the Catholic Church, and it was interesting to start to learn more about each other. He starting to feel more protective toward her. He felt in a way that she was like his child; or that they were children together. He saw her as she was, sometimes as a child. Isn't that marvelous, that lovers can be all ages for each other. Sometimes he felt forty-three, other times he was like sixteen, then he'll slip into being two. She thought it was the most exciting thing in the world, to look over at someone you thought was really cool and know they wanted to spend the rest of their life with you.

Walker got moved over into her condo in the city. The Berkeley house that Walker rented with his classical Deadhead roommate—it was a fine old place that was a lumber baron's folly down on 7th Street—was closing down. (They had held some wonderful dances in that place, dancing on beautiful blonde mahogany hardwood plank flooring in front of towering speakers). His roommate was buying his own condo and it was time for Walker to make the move to the city. So, a little while before the wedding, Walker moved his small home office into the extra bedroom in Sam's condo. Sam's neighborhood had an awful lot of people dealing crack on the street corners. But it was close to the 280 for making work runs down to Silicon Valley.

And right away he was into a new job at Apple. He made the commute down the 280 to Cupertino everyday. Looking over at Crystal Springs reservoir, formed where several faults collided, was a highlight of his trip. It was pretty, sailing through the curvaceous rolling green hills over the Stanford Linear Accelerator and past the parabolic dish. It was great working at Apple; it was so stimulating that it made him feel like he was in graduate school. The average age seemed to be no more than 25. A predominance of women in the mid-level management pool made it into a matriarchy. It was stimulating to be around these very bright creative people. One programmer he worked with had a couple of computers on his desk, would be typing away in some programming language then would turn around a play a bluesy riff on his digital sampler piano. He'd rock out for a bit, then swivel back around and type on his program. He was into some kind of mind heightening meditation discipline community and was an all-around good guy.

Things were really looking up for Walker. He was on a euphoric high. There is nothing like having your archetypes meshing. Walker started going with Sam to her choir and singing with them in the front of the church. Marriage was going to make him a much nicer person. A regular guy.

Just before the wedding Walker met Sam's parents. They were very old people. They had married late, and had waited a long time to have Samantha. Her father was delighted when Sam told them they were getting married. He leaped out of his chair, took Walker's hand in both of his hands, shook it vigorously and shouted with gratitude, "FINALLY! Thank god!"

Since Sam was a modern woman of independent means—owned a condo and her own business—she wanted a prenuptial agreement. That gave Walker pause. He absolutely loathed and detested the whole idea of prenuptial agreements. He had heard his buddies teasing about it: "She's got him on CONTRACT, man." What does it say about love and romance and marriage and commitment in the modern age of me-first. But maybe there was something to it. Try to put yourself in her place, he said to himself. When you think about it, we do come from the "free love" generation, a generation of go-go dancing, binge-drinking, pot-smoking, amoral collegiate hipsters, making love and not war whenever possible. Because it was safe—there was birth control and antibiotics. A nice quiet long marriage was the last thing we needed. About love he had always thought: It was better to want what you do not have than have what you do not want. Walker looked at the situation with his own parents: My parents stuck together for the sake of the kids. And they were miserable. I can't count the amount of door slamming and "Fine!" exclamations that belied their acting ability. I think most marriages grow unhappy and become like that. And yet you would never imagine things turning out that way to look at my parents' wedding picture. It is the picture of youthful hope and confidence. He looks exceeding spiffy in short hair and double breasted suit. Her dress is simple and elegant, her hair done up high in that 40's style with a big floppy bow in it like a star from the movie magazines. There they are, captured forever: a man and a woman walking down the aisle of a church having just been married. He has a suit of the finest cloth and she has a slim little suit made of pale blue crepe. It has an open collar; it is cosmopolitan and urbane. She is holding a bouquet of flowers in her gloved hands. They were young lovers. He is handsome and he is looking over at her in the most endearing way. And in fact is a little surprised, as they walk arm in arm out of the frame directly toward you into the future. Though his eyes turn toward her with undeniable admiration and satisfaction at his good fortune, she is looking straight ahead, holding a small corsage of flowers at her waist with her right hand, gloved to the elbow; and her left hand is hooked through his proffered right arm. She had a look of slight shyness and yet triumph in her smile. They walk, they sojourn, they stride, with that long reaching step of jitterbug dancers. They are so competent. He's a young sailor now but has graduated from university, in chemistry, with a great future. It was a cold gray day, December the first, 1946. The War was over. Their generation had really done something. And they stepped out the door of the church in Montreal to a world of hope and so much sunshine to come.

I came along pretty soon and I got to have the divine couple to myself, for a little while. I remember the handsome young couple jitterbugging in the kitchen. Whoo, what a rumble that was. Swinging through the jungle on a linoleum floor. He would hold her above him while she kicked her legs out, then she would slide way down between his legs, and he would pull her back up and throw her again. Yes, that's the people I come from.

They never believed that, what—this distance, this familiarity, when you stop being lonely, when you stop needing money, when your kids are grown is going to settle in. They didn't have any love insurance. They didn't need it. The were sure. They were people who signed on for the long haul. When my parents entered marriage, the thought would never have occurred to them that they will break up. But since then the statistics have changed: lots, if not most, marriages don't last. How *does* one go into marriage facing those statistics. It was a risk.

It made Sam wonder too: Is this why I am getting married? To get away from my mother's house and enter into Grownupsville, population everyone else?

Walker told himself is was a good exchange. Women who have children live longer. Men who are married live longer. Were they any happier? That remains to be seen.

Sure they were getting married because of the money, the children, the creation of family, the struggle to flee loneliness, to have someone to confront the fear with, to have someone to hang in with you through the desperation, to help you fulfill your familiar and biological obligation. And yet more reasons for Walker: she was the dark haired beautiful woman of his dreams, the one who turned him on, and who made him feel fairly normal.

Sam thought getting married was like getting a job she really wanted. A job where you will be working in the realm of commitment to each other. She wondered if she and he would still be the place you wanted to come to at the end of each day, after the butterflies had gone. If so, then that would be love. Because true love is in that stillness where you can spend the rest of your life with someone else. It was worth the work.

Walker got philosophical about it. Getting married, as the old master Jung might tell you, is about modeling marriageability, it is about archetypal sub-personalities—the anima and the animus—meshing. That's what gets you attracted, but then can you stay with it after those archetypes release their hold on you. You see, when we were coming up, our idea of what we are going to love in a potential mate gets formed based on what we experience with our parents. Boys marry their mothers, girls marry their fathers. Or an aspect of their mother and father that they see and became fixated upon, aspects of there parents that they took and combined with other aspects until this composite is built, and they called it god. Marriage was about reconstituting the group called family, and in that group to martial the projections needed to fight off the invading hordes for the rest of our lives. This group is held together by the shadow. The shadow is the ability to organize anger against a threat, and martial that anger in a way that we come to perceive that threat as sub-human or otherwise abominable. My shadow has to becomes *your* shadow. And if it doesn't, then I might project my shadow on you; or you on me. It is a precarious affair. And if we can do it, it means that you can trust. That in this big wide world of unknowns, someone really has got your back. Permanently. Someone is looking out for you, caring about you, making sure you're okay, and you are saying that you are committed to doing the same for that someone else.

Walker decided: maybe it's superstition, maybe it's just premonition, maybe it is ill-feeling from a lifetime of feeling rejected by women, but this girl has got her heart set on this project and who am I to stand in the way. I'm not going to refuse to marry Sam because she wants a prenup. The race would never get the new world started if that was the deal breaker.

Sam got some kind of form from her lawyer, and worked it up. It started plainly: This is a prenuptial agreement entered into by WALKER UNDERWOOD and SAMANTHA MAJESKI, freely and without reservation, as follows. And it was broken down into Real Property and Businesses and Creative Works. Since she already owned the condo, Walker wanted to make sure that the proceeds of any sale went to her. Since she had her own business, the bookstore, Walker wanted to make sure she knew he had no interest in that. And since Walker had his own interface design business, he wanted to keep that separate. Since is was very important to him, Walker did get a clause in about nurturance and support of creative work. And ownership of copyright. On paper they did indeed look like they were planning on collaborating.

Walker had terminated his psychotherapy.

Getting married was like jumping from the 10,000 foot level. And his fall was accelerating faster and faster into take-off into a new life.

The day of their wedding they got up together, in her condo. He had bought a new suit for the occasion. (He almost didn't get the pants in time from Stonestown Mall down 19th Avenue.) She wore a little white suit. The wedding service took place in a little Catholic church.

The wedding ceremony had a quote from Baal Shem Tov (whoever that was): "From every human being there rises a light that reaches straight to heaven, and when two souls that are destined to be together find each other, their streams of light flow together, and a single brighter light goes forth from their united being." It was important to her, and nice. Walker got a quote from good old e.e. cumings into it: Love is more thicker than forget / more thinner than recall / more seldom than a wave is wet / more always than never.

Love is the ultimate leap of faith. From the 10,000 foot level Walker fell all the way through the wedding and when he landed he found himself sitting at the wedding party in which he and his new wife Sam, Samantha Antonia Majeski, were the hosts and guests of honor. Her parents were there, they were footing the bill, it was a $2000 party in an uptown walnut paneled restaurant. Walker's sister Karen had flown in from Texas. The choir from Sam's church had joyously sung to one of their own. In attendance were mostly a few of her friends. KP was there with Lucia, he was the best man.

The thing Walker remembered upon waking up from the fall was how the waiters came in with neat little brushes and swept up the crumbs from the first course of the wedding feast. Later his new wife whispered in his ear that he needed to go around to the other tables and make conversation. Which he did.

Modeling Marriageablity

Urbance

Moving from the rarefied air of Berkeley to the urban density of San Francisco was somewhat of a shock for Walker. He had a hard time getting use to Sam's neighborhood. It was heavily infested with crack dealers. Walker had to rent a little studio in the 'hood about four blocks away from their condo in order to free up the spare bedroom to make way for the baby. They converted that room to a nursery with a lovely wooden crib, a chest of drawers, a changing table, and a fine old toy chest made by Sam's father. Walker moved his desk, computers, and AV equipment into his new office.

Going to work at his contractor's office required traipsing past a gauntlet of crack dealers posturing and maneuvering for deals on every corner. They had a way of looking into every passing car that told you of an edgy readiness for violence. Walker felt anxiety at the urban sprawl, but it was an exciting, creative time in computers. Walker had his own software company, a little consulting firm. As a Technical Writer he felt like the Knight Errant of technology going from job to job, riding in on your white horse to do the things others couldn't. Prowling the integrated circuit landscape of Silicon Valley for so many years, he had come to know Sunnyvale and Palo Alto and Mountain View as well as old Berkeley. Now, though, he was centered in crack alley.

The cops started cracking down on the crackheads. One day they chased one of the street dealers, causing him to jump the fence and run up the back stairs of the place where Walker rented his studio. The guy ran right through the open kitchen door into the house. The owner was downstairs, and hearing the commotion upstairs, said, "What the hell?" Then he opened the front door and saw this huge Negro standing at the head of his stairs. The owner jumped back and bolted himself into the other downstairs apartment. Then there were cops outside—a man and a woman cop, and they eventually trapped and arrested this crack dealer inside the house!

Whenever he was between clients, Walker took the opportunity of unemployment to do some of his own writing. For Walker, the perfect writing was in the intimacy of a letter to a loved one. He imagined the perfect reader, someone intelligent that you wanted to touch and beguile and edify, someone you could play with in your humor, someone you could trust to let know you.

Walker's methodology started with writing about a memory of himself in the first person. Then he rewrote the incident from the first person point of view of *another* character in the incident, thus looking at his own self from outside. Then he changed the whole thing to the omniscient POV. Along the way, he added much scaffolding—design criteria and lyrical energy requirements—and fulfilled them. It was a laborious process. He used literature as a deep feedback system to pursue enlightenment.

Walker longed for an *instrument* for writers to play the way musicians do. He started to develop one in software. It was based on the paradigm of Writer as Game Master in the RPG (role-playing game) fantasy world. He called his software instrument GameWriter. It was a general visual database for writers and game masters to pour all their notes and research into. GameWriter explores the idea of the game as metaphor for the process of writing, since writing heroic fiction and fantasy role-play adventure gaming is similar. It was a game playing / interactive simulation approach to writing. It was part outliner, part idea processor, part writing tool, part database, part creativity brainstorming tool. He even thought to make it collaborative, networkable for the (on-line, bulletin-board, multi-user, dungeon) computer game, or the classroom. GameWriter was a shell database and word processor, into which you collect the specific details of your game world. It even invoked a random number generator to simulate dice toss to test interaction outcomes and to populate cannon-fodder soldier characters with attributes. To give a concrete illustration of GameWriter's capabilities, Walker developed a database in it around Cyberpunk, a type of science fiction and a kind of role-playing fantasy game. This database takes material from current events and the novels of cyberpunk science fiction like *Neuromancer*, as well as popular Cyberpunk role-playing game systems. Since it used HyperCard's visual interface to access this data, Walker called it HyperCyberpunX. The X was there because it is like an expert system in the sense that it is an interactive knowledge base, it embodies rules, it performs tests, it queries assumptions, and simulates outcomes. (And the end-cap looked vaguely tortured and rebellious there at the end of its name.) HyperCyberpunX.

Right about that time, there was that horrendous shoot-out at a Good Guys store in Sacramento. It was a night of horrific violence captured for all the world to see on national TV, enough to displace the footage of heavily armed Marines riding around in Humvee assault vehicles fighting the Gulf War. Walker, who had never owned a TV set when he lived in Berkeley, wondered: What kind of a world was he bringing children into? What forces had conspired to make this insane tragedy happen—four members of the Oriental Boys gang in Sacramento took over a Good Guys electronics store. Walker couldn't tear himself away from CNN. The boys didn't intend to rob the store, they were just really angry about not being able to find any work. There were three brothers aged 17, 19, and 21, and a friend aged 23. They decided they were going to force the American government to fly them to Thailand where they could fight communists. They might have been up on some drugs—zombium maybe, made them think they were invisible, or impermeable to bullets. More than likely, it was their rage at not being taken seriously in the negotiations with the police—macho rage will overcome all fear of death. Is that it?

In real time, the news showed the SWAT team

storming the store, live on national TV. The gunmen had the hostages, bound hand and foot, lined up in a row in front of the glass doors at the front of the store. A police sniper's bullet missed a gunman enraging him, and he went down the line shooting as many of the hostages, at point-blank range, as he could. You could see their bodies bounce with the impact of the bullets. God it was awful.

Walker began to wonder how he would have acted in the store—with the four terrorist gunmen tying up hostages and holding guns to their head. What would he have said? Would he be street-wise enough to cool them out? To at least stay their hand, save himself?—when they were flipping coins and playing enie, meanie, miney mo with the lives of the forty-one hostages?

Walker somehow wanted to use his writing to key up his senses to be more aware of the level of violence he felt in his neighborhood. And he wanted to work with the new software he had just created. Of course, as always, Walker is a disciple of Kerouac, in that he puts the people he loves into his stories. Writing, for Walker, was an attempt to hold these loved ones closer. So he set out to write about some of his friends and his wife and worry about them getting into violence, because he knows each of them as real people. He would use violence in his writing to pare away the physical flesh and enable the soul (or is it spirit?) of the character to flower. He wanted to use violence in a spiritual way. And, now that he was married, he was feeling the pressure to make something to sell and sell quickly! Either the story or the software. Or both. Since only violent things sold, Walker decided to write this story:

Urban Angst at the 7-11 in 2019. It had his wife and friends in it. And it had the magic of the old warehouse theatre at 2019 Blake in Berkeley.

Urban Angst at the 7-11 in 2019

They are coming in off a run, Joe Swan and his gang. Cruising through the landscape of a modern city in a typical Humvee, urban, light-assault vehicle that comfortably seats the five people. Joe Swan is riding shotgun, his wife Sam driving. Wild Bill in the seat behind him; Roux is in the seat next to Wild Bill. And KP is further in the back in the next row of seats with Shep, the dog. Joe Swan is looking out his side window at the decaying urban landscape. The Bay Area metrosprawl of 2019 is home to over fifty million human beings. Cities are interconnected campuses of the megacorporations separated by walls from the Blocks. The corporate campuses are as big as small cities, with their own governments and security and much better density-to-light ratios. Moving among the Blocks, you saw endless rows of twelve to fifteen-story buildings against a swastika zigzag of sky.

Just going down to the local 7-Eleven could be dangerous in 2019. The world is so violent that everybody drives armor-plated cars or big heavy-duty vans, all with four-wheel drive and able to roll over broken glass and twisted steel. The vans are called technicals, and even though they do not have big machine guns mounted outside, they still carry a lot of fire power inside. People move through the maze of the metrosprawl between the electronic doors of their home compounds to the secure parking lots of their destinations.

Joe Swan is thinking about his bid for the current contract. The whole team had just been to visit Mr. Johnson of Encephalodyne Corporation, a giant conglomerate into electronics, semiconductors, bioengineering, and so forth. They wanted Swan to find somebody, an engineer and designer who had walked off with the only prototypes of some new chips. Encephalodyne was developing Magic chips. These chips could sense the presence of Magic and be used to manipulate it. Apparently they worked and had the people at Encephalodyne spooked, otherwise why would they need Joe Swan and his group of shadow runners to get those chips back?

Joe Swan and his gang: Wild Bill, Roux and KP, with Sam, Joe Swan's wife, driving, as usual—she is an excellent driver—is heading back into their home zone. Suddenly Sam activates the vehicle's computer with a switch on the steering column.

"I'm hungry. I gotta have somethin' to eat—bad," she says. The lovely Sam. She is so vulnerable. In the future, there are so many people that life expectancy is not long, and not very many women get pregnant. It is positively a heroic act. Pregnant women wear special kevlar, barrel-shaped, body vests that can not be penetrated even by teflon-tipped armor piercing bullets. The stylish young woman of 2019 can peruse catalogs devoted to the latest in bulletproof fashions and maternity wear.

The digital terrain map in a little monitor on the dashboard flashes a couple of lights, close to the icon of their van. The words: "7-Eleven, turn right at the second exit, go 4 blocks" advance across a bulletin board reader. Sam changes lanes and heads for the convenience store.

"Yep. Gotta feed the pregos," Joe Swan teases.

Sam pokes him in the arm. The sensitive kevlar material of his faux leather jacket instantly coalesces around the point of impact, becoming hard enough to stop a bullet.

Joe Swan feels lucky to be married to Sam. Most people in 2019 are married and/or are in closed group marriages. There are so many deadly virulent sexual diseases about that, in order to have any kind of variety in their sexual behavior, people live in strict group marriages. There is one disease that immediately causes the penis to calcify and fall off upon contact with vaginal secretions. A lot of people are into teledildonics and stimsim.

The sun is just setting when the crew pulls into the 7-Eleven for some snacks. With its three cars and a van, the lot looks tame enough. The crew will not be lugging when they go in. They don't have metal detectors in these doorways, and it's just as well, because they wouldn't get any business if they did. Besides, many guns have a stealth version made of cast ceramic with a chemical firing mechanism and no metal parts. Still the shadow runners leave the heavy artillery—the assault rifles, grenade launchers, SAMs, and Uzzis—in the van with old Shep, a yellow lab. Shep is a gun dog.

KP had saved Shep's life when he took him from a lab where horrible experiments had been done on him. Shep had video camera lenses instead of eyes, so that what the dog's "eyes" told the dog's brain could be intercepted and broadcast to closed-channel video receptor glasses that his master wore. Shep had a chemical sense detector that could be tuned for a particular smell. Worst of all, thin, small-caliber metal gun barrels had been inserted up each of Shep's nostrils making him into a remote, chemically-triggered gun dog that could be fired either interactively or by setting some threshold to trip. Taken care of by both Wild Bill, whom dogs love and who loves dogs, and KP, who is a mechanical whiz, Shep is oblivious to it all and still wags his tail, happy in the eternal adolescence of dogness.

They have to make a dash across the lot in the rain, Joe Swan assisting Sam who has swollen up like a pumpkin, holding her elbow even though she is quite capable. Upon entry, he steps out of the way and holds the door open for the rest of his crew to pass.

First, Sam—she is 5'6, lanky, with long dark hair and startling dark brown eyes; outrageously good-looking in a youthful way. As an only child, she became very good at marketing herself and usually got her way. Joe Swan tries to grab his wife and kiss her as she passes by him, but she gives him a perfunctory kiss, and says, "Don't get between a pregnant lady and her burrito."

Then Roux, his brother, who has recently gone into a Sufi phase and is wearing a top hat and tails, and, like a Gypsy, dances all the time. He would go into a twirl at any given opportunity. Roux is a petite elegant man, with a high oval pate in front of a receding hair-line. He has insisted the crew call him by his new street name—Fred. He is carrying a Colt American L36, because he can hide the sleek profile of this slim-line 6-shot automatic in his bulletproof cummerbund.

Then KP enters, a big tall engineer, who is slightly overweight, and has a beard. He wears a bullet proof flack jacket with lots of pockets. He carries an Aries Predator in a custom-fitted holster under his arm. That was the way the detectives did it, and if it was good enough for them it was good enough for KP.

Wild Bill has to stoop to avoid bumping his head on the top of the doorway. He is a big bull Ork nearly 8 foot tall, over 300 pounds, whose lower canines curl up over his top lip. Built like a cigarette machine, he has no neck and looks bad as hell. He has long, LONG sloping shoulders, making him appear as if his hands hung down almost to his knees. And his hands—he has hands with fingers like big dicks. A powerful lithe metahuman—actually an emergent species called *robustus,* a variation on *sapiens*—he is as much an expression of pure genetics as a habit of wild life and weight lifting. He can easily squat 1,000 pounds. He is attractive in a rugged masculine sort of way, has a large meaty and sweetly bovine face. He even sports a ring in his nose. Since he recently fell in love and has been busy in his relationship, he has cut off all that hair and taken to wearing expensively tailored, 1930s, double-breasted Mafia-style suits. The rest of the crew kid him about being a "brute in a suit." He likes the heavily-oiled Italian rat look. He wears his hair short and slicked down, is always dapper. He sports a rose in his button hole, and masks his heavy Ork odor with liberal dousings of after shave. There is something almost dainty in the way he moves, it is so efficient.

Joe Swan enters last. He is 6 foot 3 and always manages to look collegiate in a biker sort of way: white shirts and jeans under a heavy leather motorcycle jacket. He is carrying a 9mm Glockenspiel in a holster on his arm. It is a smart gun. All he has to do is point his finger at somebody, and tap his thumb on his ring and—fast, the gun comes down his sleeve holster into his hand, and fires itself at the target point the smart goggles were focusing on. They take a digital image of the eye as it focused, then an image of what the eye was looking at. The system does a computer enhanced comparison of these two. All you have to do is get the gun more or less pointed in the direction of the target. The system automatically takes over and fine tunes the aiming and firing so that the shot hits the pixel at the center of the target. Basic philosophy of the street is, you must have smaller, better, faster equipment than your competitor and suffer not the scum to live.

Joe Swan has to admire his team of shadow runners, especially Wild Bill, one of his oldest friends. He is a first generation Ork who has undergone the painful process of meta-humanization brought on by random rapid evolutionary effects of the UnRestricted Genetic Expression (URGE) that passed like a wave through the population of the world during the time of Coming Through. This genetic plague changed every tenth individual into an Ork, an Elf, or a Troll. It was a process of metamorphosis so painful that many didn't survive, and of those who did, many were deranged. The URGE struck teenagers shortly after the onset of puberty. Normal children might start to sprout horns, or their bone structure and musculature could change in a couple of days. Wild Bill's parents had the good sense to give him over to be raised by Comanche aboriginals, who were able to channel, transform, and refine the psychoses and aberrant behavior patterns, concomitant with meta-humanization, such that he was socialized fairly normally. What's more, being raised by Comanches, Wild Bill became a Warrior in service of nature.

And nature had gone haywire. Nature had been

stretched to capacity and time had grown thin and wrinkled. You couldn't take a shortcut, or make a beeline. People only did things in quick fixes, putting out fires created by things that got put off. Deadlines became asymptotic, ever receding mirages . . . Beginning sporadically in the 1980s and increasingly before and after the new millennium, time became logarithmic, oscillatory, and discontinuous. The newspapers had started calling this period in the history of humankind—Coming Through.

Around the turn of the millennium, Earth entered a highly non-linear gravitation wave traveling through our arm of the galaxy. The universal constant of gravity, Big-G—which Dirac had predicted was neither constant nor universal but eroded slowly due to the expansion of the universe—entered a zone of instability. This resulted in a situation much like the phases of water changing states between ice and steam. If the latent heat of fusion—that plateau at the change-over point between these two states of matter was not constant but fluctuated, what would happen to the normal progression of events at the state-change? Similarly, when the constant of gravity began to fluctuate, there occurred phase changes between space and time. Space is like the steam of time, and matter is like the ice of time. It turns out that in the fine structure of time, there is something like a latent heat threshold between local domains of time in which events can either move slower and slower, becoming logarithmic and asymptotic, so that no matter how much energy you put into an action, the closer you got to completion of an endeavor, the longer and longer it seemed to take. Or alternately, like water condensing into ice, time can become compressed and events and states undergo condensation in an instant. These were catastrophes and accidents. It was all rather horrible and confusing. One reaction the human brain had to Coming Through time was narcolepsy. Going on the nod. Narking off. People would just go blank, pull inside themselves for a while. But nodding off alone is very dangerous, and that's why it was necessary to always travel in groups.

Lately, Joe Swan had realized his group of shadow runners was so stable because it was built on the basic four types necessary to form a complete group. This went back to the most basic hunting group of ancient times: the Hunter, the Athlete, the Shaman, and the Clown. The Hunter knew all about the game, knew how to read the signs and track, knew about camping and survival. The Athlete was the one in the best physical shape. With only primitive death tools of poisoned sticks, it was necessary for the hunting group to track wounded game for days, sometimes weeks. The Athlete could cut several days off their hard trek by chasing down a wounded animal. The Shaman was along, then as now, to check out the omens and spiritual energies. And the Clown would enliven the hunting party, for the trek was often long and arduous.

Of course, things and needs are quite different now. The Clown is not so much necessary to cheer up the adventurers on a long journey, but more for his topsy-turvy perspective. It turns out this is of real value, for in the world at the beginning of the new millennium, things kind of ran together in some ways and were very spaced out in others. In Joe Swan's group of shadow runners, each can take on more or less any role, but generally Wild Bill is the Athlete, Roux the Clown, Joe Swan the

Shaman, and KP the Hunter.

Wild Bill is the athlete, the warrior, the most physical, the one who knows the most about violence. KP is the Hunter, the technical whiz, the hacker. To tease him, when he is being overly self-contained and it appears aloof or being overly thoughtful and circumspect, the group sometimes calls him Mad Dog. When it comes to hacking, KP has pit-bull chops. He sinks his bytes into something and won't let go until he has it. He is famous for once typing nonstop on a keyboard for 25 hours straight. He didn't even stop to go to the bathroom, but peed into a bottle, all the while keeping himself up on doughnuts and Jolt cola. Roux is the Clown, or more, the poet, for he looks at perfectly ordinary things in marvelous ways and at strange and terrifying things in ordinary ways. Thus, it fell upon Joe Swan to be the Shaman, though he was not a shaman, really. He had studied physics, and this prepared him to cross over the line and dabble in metaphysics. He is the serious member of the group who reads signs and omens and generally observes things with a parental countenance.

A new type has evolved called Drivers, who never nark out, and Sam is one of them. She is always capable of putting one foot in front of the other and carrying on, no matter what.

Concomitant with Coming Through time, Magic officially came back into the world. The date recognized for this watershed is June 30, 1998, in Waco, Texas. At that particular moment in time, Waco became for a while the largest concentration of physical and mental energies on the planet. While the Waco physicists at the 54 mile Extremely Strong Interaction Ring were doing their experiments and sharing their results across the

Internet, the Comanche Indians there performed the ceremony of the Great Medicine Wheel—they were hosting a world-wide gathering of the tribes, at which indigenous peoples from all over the world shared ancient knowledge of nature and the spirit. The Dalai Lama was present with a retinue of monks the size of a whole monastery.

It was luck that Joe Swan was doing graduate physics work at the superconducting super-collider site in Waco, under the directorship of Emmanuel Elle-Mann, the famous French neo-Cartesian physicist from CERN, and it was luck that Joe Swan met Wild Bill there, but it was no coincidence Magic emerged at that time (though our theories of coincidence and synchronicity are much changed now, too).

Astrophysicist noticed the entrance of our world into the epoch of Coming Through time first. The signs of the chaotic breakdown of the fabric of space-time first appeared when the background radiation of space left over from the Big Bang cooled from 2.73 degrees to 2.718 . . . and became transcendental. The Waco facility produced a 2.718 erg energy beam that provided the necessary filament thread to attract and precipitate out a steady state emergence of the new particles. It turned out the beam could be seen in higher dimensions as a thread which began an irreversible thermodynamic process, like precipitating a crystal out of a supersaturated solution. Thus began the emergence of a new kind of matter into our local observable dimension. The hunt for Magic quarks was on. And the aboriginals saw it, too. The American Indians were the first to make contact with Magic. What's more, they were able to harness it. In fact it could be controlled by the age old techniques of their ancient wisdom. The rigorous and tortuous path of knowledge the traditional shaman or sorcerer travels is just what is needed to become able to withstand and channel these forces.

With its experimental production by physical science, magic got the official stamp of approval. It became the fifth force, after gravity, electromagnetism, and the strong and weak interactions. Magic came to be seen as nature's way of empowering the indigenous peoples of the earth. This, at last, insured Nature herself became a voice to be heard at the Council of Nations. By the end of the 90s, bio-regionalism had become a big part of politics. One good result of all this turmoil was the movement toward concilience economics. The social and environmental sciences became quantifiable empirical sciences and starting with all government contracts, the dimension of environmental costs were equitably, perspicaciously factored into every expenditure.

As part of his graduate work in physics, Joe Swan had to conduct ethnobotanical and anthropological field research, doing interviews among the Indians. Joe Swan and Wild Bill became friends.

The way Wild Bill said it: "Magic is about Spirit. Spirit is magic getting in touch with flowing spirit. The hurdle to this flowing spirit is bad medicine, interference by bad use of technology, bad laws, cruelty and greed of humans, which delivers only temporary gratification. Spirit thwarted by fear or pain becomes disruptive and evil."

The way Elle-Mann said it, published in his famous paper "*Ontic Spritz*" in Physical Review: "Magic is a whole new set of quarks that are still governed by the traditional 8-fold super symmetry of invariances governing higher dimensional space." The Waco group proved that the new quarks are, of course, mass-less field quanta—bosons, like photons or neutrinos—that transmit signals from fermions—the heavy particles or nuclei. Magic was the link between dark matter, dark energy, and regular matter and regular energy.

Though it was highly unorthodox at the time, metaphysics and magic had once again become a branch of the traditional natural science curriculum and are considered mainstream now. The Waco group's methods were so unorthodox because this was man's first encounter with the co-evolutionary state-specific semiconductors. They were co-evolutionary because they could not have come into existence until this epoch, down the time line from the Big Bang, nor become observable until this point in the evolution of human consciousness. And they were state specific because, in addition to their unanticipated physical properties, the new particles possessed mental attributes as well. Observability required the observer to be in a certain state—through ingesting the right organic compounds—and required the presence of the right material, Snakesilver. Snakesilver, a heavy isotope of silver found in abundance on Io, a moon of Neptune, was mined in significant enough quantities by Encephalodyne to make magic chips.

The scientific study of these psychic quanta is possible only by researchers with strong egos. The new particles were named "demonsions" (a neologism combining demon and dimension) because the experience of observing them was more akin to demonic possession than data collection. And because, when it was realized these new particles controlled entropy and its opposite—order—they were named in honor of Clerk Maxwell's original *gedenkin* experiment on entropy, a thought experiment which postulated the existence of a being, "Maxwell's Demon." This demon could sort particles into cool and hot, thus, through a temperature differential, convert organization into energy. "We All Cogitate Ontogeny" became the Waco group's slogan.

Joe Swan's reminiscence is broken by the fluorescent whiteness of the 7-Eleven. He follows his group in, keying on Sam's every move and heading into the middle of the store. It is a relief all these stores are laid out the same. Open 24 hours a day, 365 days a year, universally the same everywhere, you can just put it on autopilot and head toward your favorite section. The fluorescent lighting gives to the aisles that same kind of unreality TV does to them.

To the left as they enter, is the check-out counter behind a solid floor-to-ceiling wall of Plexiglass, two inches thick. There is a pretty young Asian woman behind the counter. The checkout chick is absently pretty, with pale skin and hair as black and shiny as patent leather cemented back like a shellacked helmet, indicating terminal mousse abuse. To the right are four aisles, and in the second aisle is a big guy with white hair who has a large canvas bag slung across his back.

As their eyes adjust to the bright whiteness of the place, they notice more detail about the checkout counter. It has a bar code scanner, cash register terminal, credit card receptor, and various counter displays. Behind the counter is a set of stairs leading up to the manager's office. A Mr. Nicky Nicks is the manager, forty-three, short and dumpy, working in his office. A gun buff, he has a Bulldog 44 snub-nosed revolver with a laser sight on his desk.

The big dude in aisle 2 with the large shoulder bag is in his early 30s. His hair is pinched into little spikes, as if his head were a pincushion into which nails had been driven. He is dressed in a skin tight ribbed and rhindy space outfit made of leather stretched taut over huge muscles that are either artificial or suggest rampant steroid use. The right side of his face is a mask of metal and wire culminating in a lens over one eye. His name is Ben "Crackle" Guidion; he is a muscle builder type. He has a sinewy neck and a chiseled face.

Crackle, as some of the other members of his gang, the Lost Boys, call him, has a constant din in his head, which sometimes tells him what to do. He had been abused as a child and had received numerous blows to the head. The physical damage to his frontal lobes made it difficult for him to control rages. They came on him like lightning. He tried to tame the subliminal opera of his warring sub-personalities by slotting in electronic entertainment programs at all times, but these eventually eroded the neural pathways of differentiation, thus making it hard for him to distinguish hallucinatory phantasms from reality.

Sure enough, Crackle stands in the middle of aisle 2 like he is listening to some far-off melody, singing an advertising jingle for the Glockenspiel lightweight machine gun—a song that has a refrain kind of like a cheer: "Better to be judged by 12 of your peers / Than to be carried out by 6 pall bearers / Knocker socker / Cold cock that sucker / with the Glocker." Crackle has a Defiance shotgun concealed under his coat.

Joe Swan could immediately tell: this guy looks

pretty bad off; uses electronics as drugs. Perhaps no worse off than the rest of the lost, but Joe Swan made a mental note to keep a close eye on him. Too much jacking in makes hair grow on your ideas.

Sony had been first to apply electroencephalography to the entertainment industry by running the transducers backwards. They send digital signals back through the little encephalopods—the electrodes attached to various areas of the head to measure brain waves—and these signals directly stimulate the visual and auditory areas of the brain. It produces subliminal hallucinatory movies. This became a whole new kind of entertainment. Writers, working with teams of programmers and neuroanatomists, coded dreams and adventures directly into the neural nets of the brain. Reality got into it when adventurers and even murderers were able to record their sensations while committing their deeds. These recordings were sold and played on miniature synthesizers to stimulate a neural simulation of the sensations for the consumer. This new form of entertainment and electronic edification was highly addictive. The Stimsims (stimulated simulations) erased the brain/body barrier between observing and "being" the characters. However, most of the populace was not epistemologically sophisticated enough to maintain an adequate sense of self under the onslaught of this new entertainment. Just as stimsim is orders of magnitude more engaging than TV brainsuck, direct interactivity with the neural nets of the cerebral cortex is orders of magnitude more effective in controlling the population. And there were some nasty side effects.

Joe Swan, Wild Bill, Mad Dog, and Roux follow

Sam into the store past the four aisles in front of the check-out counter, turn right, and pass five aisles more until they get to the far side of the store, to aisle 10 where the refrigerated goodies are.

Wild Bill doesn't stop in front of the refrigerator but continues to the Dispenser Bar for liquid and viscous products such as Smoothies, Snorkels, HummmFree Yogurt, Jean-Paul's Malt (made with absinthe), SoyAhoy, and Soyanara, a cappuccino-like drink from Japan made with caffeine impregnated soy beans, and GlopsciousOoze, a drink prized for its mercury-like beading-up properties that dispensed with the need for a plastic cup, and so on. It also features Schwarzeneggers's Own, a high-protein malted with the double-thick option; Wild Bill loves these.

For some unknown reason, Roux spirals out of formation and goes down aisle 8 where there is a couple, Li'l Darling and Rat. Down aisle 8 on the left are candies and other megacarbohydrate satisfiers like GretaCarbos and Road Swill, which some say looks like reconstituted chunks of road kill in a bouillabaisse base. There you can find Tombstone Pizza and Tourist Mix which you actually strap over your mouth like a feed bag mask, leaving the hands free for driving. On the right is dog food. Beyond that is the bottled juice.

Li'l Darling is wearing a floor-length, bulletproof, red riding-hood, purchased out of the Victoria's Secret Armory Catalog. It is clasped around her neck with a golden chain, the hood falling down her back exposing dark hair done up in a severe bun. The floor length garment opens when she walks to reveal her costume. It is a kind of supreme retrogrunge, a darling 1890 pink pinafore several sizes too short, hovering above the tops of white stockings. Her shoulder bag contains an Aries Predator, a small, light-weight, semi-automatic machine pistol.

Li'l Darling is another of the many throwaway children, although she'd hotly deny it. Her parents are just off somewhere, that's all. Like they have been for the last 18 years, since she was found in a dumpster behind an orphanage when just a few weeks old. Fear of abandonment was a main motivating theme of Li'l Darling's mind, and it predisposed her to be very manipulative. Childhood was an endless series of torments by the older kids. She got very good at being crafty, cunning, sly, and quick. She also got good at running away and being brought back. When she was 12, she ran so far away they couldn't bring her back. The gangs were the only family she had ever felt comfortable around. There were so many things out there in the world, terrorists, cults, and just plain crazy people, that being in a gang was good for your protection. Not to mention it was necessary in case of blanking out and going on the nod. By the time she was 16, she had developed into a beauty and could control the boys with her sexual favors and play one against the other.

Rat is her current "experiment."

Enrico "Rat" Razcadiz, late 20s, is an illegal Haitian immigrant. His greasy brown dreadlocks are pulled up into a horrendous Mohawk, the long spikes rising a foot and a half off the top of his head, held up there stiff with daubed mud, a gnarly nest of twigs and pigeon feathers.

Though Rat got his training by being apprenticed to a witch doctor that specialized in zombies for sweat shops, when Rat immigrated to the US, he moved with some Sino-Amerasian Indian tribes and became a Rat

Shaman. He is an evil sorcerer, though not that powerful. This makes him paranoid and maniacal. Magic is not that good in a fire fight, too slow, so he also carries an IntraTEC DC9 9mm, another semiautomatic machine pistol. It is suspended just in reach for easy maneuverability on one shoulder strap. He also is armed with a Remington Roomsweeper shotgun suspended from a shoulder strap on his other side. They are hidden under his full-length, armor-battened poncho.

Around the corner from them, Joe Swan and Mad Dog are still trying to make their selection from the refrigerator. Joe Swan caught a glimpse of Sam handling a burrito as big as a loaf of bread as she headed back to the front counter and the Nuke and Serve section.

In the next aisle over from Wild Bill at the dispenser bar is James "Pop" Warner, early 20s but looking a decade older. Pop's face has big jowls. His sturdy pit-bull constitution is so filled with rage that he might go off half-wild at any given moment and explode—his bulging eyes bugging out even more. The Lost Boys call him "Pop" because, in addition to being leader of the gang, he is a fearless drug abuser. He has multiple addictions and will take anything, anytime, anywhere. Pop's weapon of choice is his baseball bat. He carries a canvas bat bag slung over one shoulder with an aluminum baseball bat and a set of long-handled ebony nunchuks protruding out of it. Nothing is more satisfying to him than that particular crack of a bat against the smuck-mass of a human head. His swing is so strong he could just about knock the block clean off a home-boy's shoulders; well if not clean off, he could at least decorticate his victim. He wears a bulletproof baseball uniform with knee socks and cleated shoes. On the back of his shirt is the Lost Boy's team emblem, a head being knocked out of the park by a baseball bat and coming tromp d'oile straight out the frame at you. Not all fighting is close, though, and he is armed with the Defiance semi-automatic shotgun which he caries along with several quick change ammo clips in the canvas bat-bag. He is a student of the martial arts and wears his hair tied up into a samurai topknot beneath an armored battering helmet.

Pop suffers from both jock-itch and athlete's foot and is searching among the sprays and spritzes of the personal hygiene displays in aisle 12 for Panoridalin, an all-in-one spray that will rid him of the detestable critters. The whole aisle is devoted to exterminating species that plague humans and progresses with an almost anti-evolutionary zeal, starting with anti-bacterial soaps and detergents and on to defoliants and bug sprays, fly strips, roach traps, electric UV bug zappers, gopher and mouse decapitators, ultrasonic rat dispersers, rat jails and skunk cages.

Roux wants to check out Li'l Darling and Rat. As luck would have it, a the sounds of a Viennese waltz started filling the air from the piped-in muzak coming down from the ceiling, just at that moment. Roux goes into a dance, because that is his way of seeing.

He picks up a twenty-five pound bag of dog food and begins waltzing with it down aisle 8 of the 7-Eleven, weaving and moving and feinting and advancing back and forth across the aisle. As he passes, he smiles and talks and flirts a bit with Li'l Darling. "Is it a waltz? It sort of feels like a waltz. I'd try a box step 1-23, 1-2-3, 1-2-3." Violins oceanic and lilting. "Yes, I've been learning the Vienna waltz," he says.

And he sidles up closer to the couple, moving and sliding, moving and sliding, moving and sliding. He says, "It's nice, I like the waltz, don't you? The people look like ducks, the way their feet kind of web out to the side as they move."

Li'l Darling grins at this folderol and takes it with a grain of salt; Rat is over there, his eyes as big as fried eggs, staring at her hard enough to bore holes in her skin.

Roux dances away.

Watching Roux dance is like standing next to the tracks when a huge freight train comes hurtling by. There is a rush of energy coming from somewhere, and yet it is like cinema, he can actually make you see the tone row colors of the music that he explores with his body. It's like he is taking you on a trip through the underground of a sonic city, not on a subway, rather on this graceful undulating being. You can see it! A musical entity hovering in the air! Undulating like some diurnal squeeze box of the world, or like a *Time Animal*, some huge kind of manta ray, moving through the ocean of air, invisible except for its breathing—vhah . . . vhuh . . . vhah—real slow and labored, like on a respirator. Roux goes weaving all the way down to the end of the aisle away from Li'l Darling and Rat, and when he turns the corner he sees there one Salvador "Snap" Avagadro, early 20s, of average height and medium build, all the hair shaved off his head except for a part of it spelling out "X". He wears a faux fur-lined coat with a Lost Boy's emblem on it. Snap is one of the leaders of the Lost Boys. Snap is a Scorpio and is nasty with a bull whip. He rules the gang with a personality that can shift from hot enough to thaw a cryogenic octogenarian, to cold enough to make one, in the blink of an eye. In addition to being a crack shot with the new Smith and Wesson .357 he is carrying, he is armed with a Defiance shotgun and caries three magazines of ammo.

Snap is down the aisle from where the others are looking at the refrigerated food trying to make up their minds. He is near a token fresh vegetable section toward which Mad Dog desultorily turns.

Roux is starting to see, starting to put things together, but magic is slow in these cases, you have to go into a kind of trance or sympathetic mental union with the synchronism vortex to see anything.

And he dances back up the aisle toward Li'l Darling and Rat, and sidles up to the lovely Li'l Darling who opens her little red riding hood a bit more and says, "You like the muzak?"

She catches Roux's eye and smiles, enjoying his performance. He nods to her and smiles, but cannot stop his weaving.

And Roux says, "I've got my top hat and tails in the supermarket, my hair slicked back, and I'm doing an old soft shoe."

He arches his back, dancing cheek to cheek with the bag of dog food, creating a staggering gesture within his fox trots. Walking step, side step, magic step, turn, lightly swaying and lilting with Our Lady of Dog Food. Dreaming and scheming and winging and lolling and lurching and lunging it came to him: these people are going to run amuck.

However, Roux starts to become enraptured by the beautiful time signature as he lets it take over his mind, letting the light lure him into levity; meanwhile jealousy and rage begin to take over Rat's mind.

"I'm dancing up a storm," says Roux. He springs back in triple spins, as his tails flutter out, and this incenses Rat, who pulls out his IntraTEC DC9 9mm semiautomatic machine pistol and says, "Here, maybe this will help you dance."

Rat starts firing the IntraTEC DC9 with the 30 shot clip into the shelves of juice, narrowly missing Roux as he dances past. Bullets are flying, ricocheting off cans, busting glass, exploding bottles of cranberry juice, spraying dark red fluid all up a square pillar as shells ejected into the air move in an arc and bounce around on the floor.

Li'l Darling pulls her Aries Predator out of her purse and points it at Roux. Rat scrambles up onto the top of the row of shelves, knocking everything off, and starts shooting from up there. Just for fun, Li'l Darling shoots Roux in the cummerbund.

The shot knocks the wind out of him, and he bites his tongue as he falls. There is blood in his mouth, the taste of salt. Later he would wonder if it was this ancient mixture of fear and adrenaline that released the hovering spirit. Bullets are flying all around, and Roux can't tell where they are coming from. He is trying to crawl away, but it's not easy, there is so much slick and slidey stuff on the floor now.

The manager of the store could see all this on his bank of security televisions, and it made him mad-some guy shooting up his store like that. The outraged Mr. Nicks grabs his pistol with the laser sight and goes through a little cupboard door in the wall of his office cubicle that leads out onto a maze of catwalks which runs all over the store above the ceiling tiles. He quickly climbs over the top of the Plexiglass wall and crawls onto the one he uses frequently to look down at the girls' dressing room, heading toward Rat, to put a stop to this wanton destruction by shooting Rat from above.

At that moment, three of the Lost Boys gang hit the front door, opening it with a loud BANG! and coming in fast, shouts, screams, breaking glass, shotguns and machine guns being pulled from under their clothes. They had been planning to rob the store, and when they heard the shots being fired inside, they took it as a signal to commence hostilities.

Two of them stop in front of the Plexiglass wall and start shouting and hollering at the little Asian salesgirl. "Open up the door!"

She refuses.

At the same time, the Lost Boys inside the store pull out their weapons and get the drop on the shoppers nearest to them. The gang bangers holler at the people inside the store to raise their hands and come to the front of the store. People in the place—their eyes get really wide.

The two Lost Boys open up, blasting away at the two inch thick plexiglass wall in front of the counter. The salesgirl is ducking down under her counter trying to make herself as small as possible, and screaming something in a foreign language with each shot.

The third motions for Sam, who is up front by the counter, to raise her hands.

An obese woman crouches down behind her basket and begins to scream. The frequency of her scream tips Crackle into a 'roid rage, and he runs up and starts kicking her shopping cart.

Adrenaline sets the shadow runners' teeth on edge, and they start to move, before they are even ready to move or know where they are going to move to. It is a slow motion kind of thing except it all happens very fast. They should have seen it coming, but they didn't. Wild Bill should have sensed the chemistry of their fear, but he didn't. Roux can see auras, if he'd just let his mind relax and begin to see instead of looking. Joe Swan has thermographic smart specs that can detect the infrared of heat, which he can read for aggression. Nevertheless, they all concur immediately, this gang of psychotics wants to hurt and kill people.

KP moves, ducks down one of the aisles to the right.

Snap Avagadro points his 357 magnum at him to get a shot off before KP moves out of sight.

Joe Swan's hand points and seems to just suck the pistol out of his sleeve holster into the palm of his hand and aims the gun toward the gang banger Snap's left eye. In the blink of an eye, a bullet plunges dead center into Snap Avagadro's left pupil, taking off the back of his head as it exits. At the exact same moment, a bullet shot from Snap's gun hits KP in his vest and spins him around, knocking him against a shelf.

Wild Bill, who has a big high protein malted in each fist, is confronted with Pop Warner uttering a loud "!GA!!!" Pop makes a fierce two handed baseball bat swing, bashing both malteds, splashing fluid flying everywhere. But none lands on Wild Bill, who is as fast as he is big. The warrior with the top knot starts going crazy and chasing Wild Bill around with his big bat. Wild Bill fakes him, spins around, out flanks him, and hits him a good hard one in the ribs as he goes by. The bat just whooshes past Wild Bill's ear, turning it red, as he feints back and topples over a carton of cola.

Then Joe Swan goes kind of crazy, starts shouting for Sam, turns and starts running over to where she is.

It's a good thing KP is knocked down by the shot, because he looks up and there is Rat on top of the shelf, watching Li'l Darling making Roux dance, looking down at them, pulling a Remington Roomsweeper shotgun out from under his coat as he empties the clip of the IntraTEC DC9 at Roux. Rat is turning to follow Joe Swan, as he rounds the end of the aisle and runs fast toward Sam. And just as Rat is about to shoot down Joe Swan, KP shoots Rat. Both men are saved by their bullet-proof vests. The shotgun blast that hits Joe Swan in the back launches him four feet into the air, and he crashes into the goon who is pointing a gun at Sam with enough force to knock the man down, sending the gun skating across the floor. The smart gun in Joe Swan's hand becomes entangled in its wire and dangles there, useless. KP's shot hits Rat in his bullet-proof vest and knocks him off the shelf. He slams into the opposite shelf, bounces once, hits the floor scrambling, immediately bumps into Li'l Darling who isn't too stable in her high heels, and they both fall into the aisle. Rat's shotgun butt slams into the ground and goes off as Li'l Darling falls on it. The shotgun blast hits her in the stomach. Vomit and shit slither out of her.

Rat is so enraged at the depraved state of his beloved Li'l Darling, that he levitates toward the ceiling screaming, "SHIT PISS FUCK, GOD DAMN, SON OF A BITCH! From there he can see the back of the store where Wild Bill is dodging huge swipes of the bat from Pop, he can see Joe Swan rolling around on the floor and the big goon has Joe Swan by the throat and is about to pound his face in, and Crackle is moving around them both, raising his shotgun, trying to get a dear shot at Joe Swan.

Whooma, whooma, the two goons are shooting bullets point blank into that hard Plexiglass wall that was made to keep "us in here and them out there." The shots just flake off bits of powdered plastic and bounce off, or the slug gets embedded in the plastic, sending shatter lines through it. The little Asian sales clerk behind the plexiglass wall is going nuts hunkering down behind the cash register, trying to pull her miniskirt down to cover her ass with one hand, and cover her ears with the other. The gang bangers begin cursing and laughing, yelling at her through the barrier.

"When I get ahold of you I'm gonna lay you across the counter and fuck you, hardy har har har."

And the other one is saying, "Who's gonna be first."

Round after round is being pumped into the clear plastic, the bullets tumbling and ricocheting and kicking up all kinds of sparks. There is so much firepower the plastic starts to break down with heat, a big streak running up toward the ceiling, it was shattering!

Rat goes kind of crazy and starts jumping across the store from one shelf to the next; everybody is ducking, there is this spirit in the place, something is moving and moving and keeps moving through—out of Roux, it has been conjured up by Roux. And it is on Rat's tail as he jumps across the aisles, and it starts galumping along, it is like some huge horrible manta ray, moving through the supermarket. It's spooky. Rat has the grace of the terrified as he scrambled, like some kind of wild animal running along the tops of the shelves, scattering everything down onto both sides.

There is a great big shattering crack as the plexiglass wall explodes, blasting powdered plastic everywhere, and the two goons pull the Asian salesgirl up by her slender wrist. One reaches under her skirt. About that time Mr. Nicky Nicks is in position, and after busting out a ceiling tile, places the red spot of the laser beam on the head of the one goon that has his hand up under the salesgirl's miniskirt and pulls the trigger. The bulldog 44 displaces the goon's brain, which flies out of his head, smacks the plastic door of the cigarette rack and slides down. It ends up draped like an old toupee on a hook for displaying flashlight batteries.

The salesgirl screams and the other goon grabs her, uses her as a shield. Rat screams, "KRI! AGGG BUN DOLO," and starts blasting up into the ceiling. Crackle turns his gun up there, too, and big shotgun blasts from both Rat's Roomsweeper and Crackle's Defiance hit the little manager in the guts and lift him up, he tumbles down out of the ceiling tile, except his hand gets entangled in some ducting, a bunch of electrical wires are pulled out, they started to short and spark and smoke. The manager is hung there in space.

Wild Bill is so frightened by the awful bat that Pop is swinging back and forth he makes a tremendous stretch leap. Now Wild Bill has powerful legs enhanced with gnat knee enzyme, which stores energy into a muscle giving it tremendous spring energy, enabling a gnat to jump 30 or 40 times its own length. This stuff is supposed to help Wild Bill leap over small buildings but he hasn't learned to control it too good yet, and he overdoes it and goes sailing up to the roof and over three aisles and just manages to flatten himself out like a pole vault, but, as he said later, the experience is more as if he had slid onto the back of this manta ray that was undulating through the continuum directed by Roux, toward Rat. The both of them, Wild Bill in the physical plane, and the ray in the ethereal, merge and it changes Wild Bill's trajectory as he comes over those three aisles, and Wild Bill plows into Rat, bumping the gang shaman so hard it knocks Rat into the dangling wires. There must have been a lot of juice in those wires, because when Rat hits them such a powerful electrocution processes begins that the muscles in his hand freeze, and he is unable to let go of the wires, and they snag on him, and he wiggles and dances there in the air. There is a loud pop, and all the lights in the place dim out for what seems like an eternity, and there against the blackness is a great discharge and glow around the Rat shaman like he is illumined in a flash of lightning as he screams, shocked.

It is horrible, the image of death, the two men hanging in space dangling from Mr. Nick's outstretched arm, their bodies intertwined, strapped in wires, so that they make a kind of face as the lights dim out, their two heads close together like eyes, some terribly sunken eyes, and their bodies forming the hollows of cheeks, their legs, outlining lips and forming deep furrows running through that face. And the manta settles into the "head" like a toupee, and it really does form a face that turns slowly in space.

When he saw it, Roux thought: Aww, Death has such a big sad face. Death is a face with a big ugly nose, it glows and it glowers and it hovers over the place.

But not Wild Bill. He doesn't have time for thought. For when he bounces off and crashes down from the shelves, he lands on Crackle. And in the dark, it was

Wild Bill and Crackle rolling around on the floor, and it's hand to hand, a natural genetically mutated being against the cybernetically augmented being.

Joe Swan didn't see it either. He is in a life and death struggle with the big goon on top of him who has him by the throat, and is about to smash him in the face with a big fist coming down from way up in the air, except he can't see in the dark, and when the lights settle and their eyes get used to it, Sam extrudes one of her razor knives from under the skin of the middle finger of her right hand, and quick, slashes the goon's neck cutting both the carotid artery and vein. "There mother fucker, that ought to get you offa my man," she said.

A great gout of blood gushes out of the slashed man's neck, covering Joe Swan before he could push that big goon off of him.

By now Mad Dog's mind is quiet, because he understands the layout of the place. These aisles are very protected, and he advances. As he rounds a corner, he sees Pop go by, and they both shoot each other and knock themselves back, because they are wearing bullet proof vests. But now Pop is in the line of sight of both Mad Dog and Roux, who has crawled and gotten himself up out of the sticky depravity and has drawn his Colt out, and they get Pop in a cross fire and he is shot to death instantly.

Meanwhile, Wild Bill and Crackle are slamming each other back and forth across the aisle, Crackle's hydraulic augmented grip like steel, because it is steel.

"I'm gonna fuck you up, bad man," Crackle says.

But Wild Bill twists out of it and slips around behind Crackle. With a sweep of his left foot, he trips him forward. Wild Bill gets down and puts his knee into the middle of Crackle's back and pulls up on his head until he breaks the man's neck.

It is all finished in a little over a minute.

Joe Swan is covered in blood that is wet and gross. Roux is covered in juice and degradation that is green and gooey, red and syrupy, and black and sticky. Wild Bill's suit is ruined.

"We'll have to get some counseling after this," Sam says as they walk out the door and drive off before the cops come.

Roux later said he saw bits of the souls of the dead floating up and out of the 7-Eleven, and that in the twilight sky they looked like bubbles in the amber of beer percolating up and out of the city, beginning a journey across some great divide.

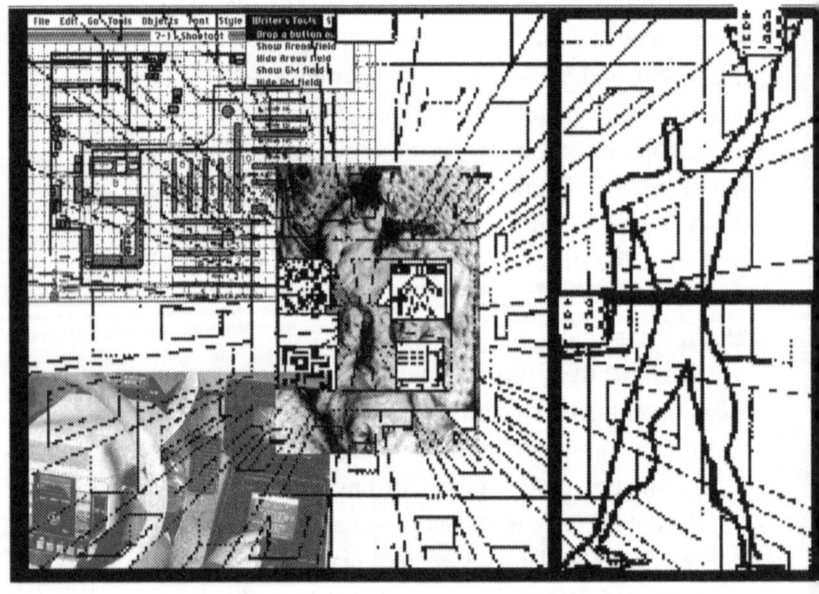

Bring It On

"EEEEEYARRRG!" Sam was not happy. She complained, "I was so tired I almost pitched forward and fell asleep in my *pasta.* I got to bed and must have passed out into sleep at some point. I was talking to Joan and I totally passed out. I even woke up tangled in my own phone when the alarm went off. I'm sick of being so Pregnant!"

She looked all addled and caged.

"I feel like hell up a tree. My stomach is so huge, I feel like a blimp (whine, whimper, sniffle). My ears are ringing and my back aches. UGH. I HATE being pregnant so much. I want to go out and see my friends. I want to take part in the action and the passion of the times, or at least follow this election."

Walker knew that politics and elections were very important to Sam. He felt like such a blunt for not even being a citizen, and unable to give her much of a political conversation.

She said, "I want to go to Mooses and be with my Democratic club and wait for the election results to be posted and broadcast from city hall."

Sam was a founding member of the Snotty Bitches Association, a moderately successful Democratic political club and kvetch association, navigating the cut-throat, viper-ridden world of San Francisco democratic intrigue with the help of her impressive and ever-expanding collection of political shit-disturbers. Their motto was: Shit Happens But We Don't Have To Take It. They regularly got together, usually in Mooses, or the Washington Square Bar and Grill (known as the Washbag) or other famous political watering holes around San Francisco during elections and campaigns. The Washbag and Mooses were on opposite sides of Washington Square, the heart of North Beach, at the center of the old Italian, Irish Catholic political scene there. Even Da Mayor, Willie Brown hisself, ever a staunch Democrat had—before he became no longer a man of the people—allowed himself to be an honorary inductee into the Snotty Bitches Association Democratic Club.

Walker said, "Well, you can't go out by yourself. I'll take you. But I won't be able to sit at the table with the 'ladies.' When they get you and Dianne, and Barbara and Vicky together it is like 'Estrogen Overload Central.'"

Sam smiled.

Walker pulled up in front of the bright window at Mooses, double-parked with his flashers on, got out, ran around, held her door open and helped Sam out. A doorman ushered her in from there as Walker told her, "After I park the car, I'm going down to City Lights to read. You can page me there if you need to. I'll be back here to get you in TWO HOURS. OK?"

"OK."

Inside Mooses, the sea of swell people parted like the Nile before her body, wide with child, and the table of women friends got up and reshuffled themselves to give her the queen seat. Holding court at their table on election night, it was Dianne, Barbara, Sam and Vicky waiting for the results of the district run-off to come in. It felt good to be in that upscale environment; the starched white tablecloths, the loud scrape of chrome chairs on tile floors, the hustle of waiters, and the roving, table-hopping of broad, expansive, glad-handing, stuffed-shirt politicians on the make had an aura of power. The Snotty Bitches were drinking a pitcher of Margaritas. Sam said, "Since I'm pregnant, I'm not drinking." She ordered a Coke.

Dianne, the head of the Snotty Bitches Association, was a hopelessly tall, bossy woman who is dedicated and active in community affairs. She was a journalist and an editor of a political magazine Taking Control. Sam was somewhat envious and somewhat disdainful of Dianne, because Dianne's father, a very rich man, had supported her through her twenties and thirties while she interned at a Time Magazine bureau. This enabled Dianne to "earn" her job as editor through the time-honored tradition of trust fund. Vicky was Vicky Wong, a bureaucrat in the San Francisco Department of Human Resources who made sure everybody dotted their i's and crossed their T's on applications. Barb was now an entrepreneur with her own business, a woman's sex shop called Come As You Are.

The last time they had been together, Sam was just back from getting married. They had teased her unmercifully when she told them she was getting married. Though many of them had been married and some of them had children, they were all un-married now.

Now the whole country was on a tear about the Clinton and Monica scandal in the White House, and very quickly the ladies availed themselves to the opportunity to vent their vexation over the situation.

Barb: "They ought to rename the Oval Office the Oral Office."

Dianne: *(read face bursting with mirth)*: "No kidding, man. *(She clears her throat and launches into an oratory.)* Security system: 50 million dollars. Fine Cuban cigar (that you get past contraband): $100. Keeping Yasser Arafat on hold during another Middle East crisis while you get a blow job from an intern: Priceless."

This cracked everyone up.

Sam: "And that Linda Tripp. What a trip *she* is. How would you like to have a so called quote, friend, unquote that recorded your conversations."

Vicky: "And that hair on her! What is going on in that woman's mind? What are her mirrors made of?"

Sam: "Well, if it wasn't for her I guess we wouldn't EVEN know about it."

Barb: "Yes, the poor dear lovely Monica Lewinsky of the raven-hair, was *so confused* that she had to spill her guts to somebody."

Dianne: "I bet there'll be lots of little female White House staffers suddenly remembering that they too have been improperly propositioned by the president at some time."

Vicky: "I wonder if he propositioned the page-*boys* as well."

Barb: "Naaa. That good ole-boy is strictly a nookie hound."

There were titters all around.

Dianne: "There's been sexual allegations dogging

him ever since he was in politics. It looks like the guy is a serial philanderer."

Sam: "Serial philanderer. Ha, ha. That's a good one."

Dianne: "Now, they are getting rid of him. Well this is a very moral, or should I say oral, country."

Sam: "And that Geraldo Rivera! God, I can't stand that guy. I was watching that show of his the other night, Geraldo Rivera, Live. But I guess it is taped."

Barb: "Basically what he says is: 'Lying about sex isn't lying.' *Duuuhh.* What a worm."

Later Barb started in on her feminist agenda with Sam. "You are going to teach him about the natural superiority of women, aren't you."

Barb: "I grew up in a very pro-Womyn family with a Mother who is a strong Feminist and who taught me to appreciate the natural strength and authority of women. I see women as the naturally superior gender and so it is natural for me to support their empowerment."

Sam: "Superior gender?"

Dianne: "From a biological perspective, certainly. Women live longer, heal faster, have a greater pain threshold. . ."

Barb: "And they are way more powerful sexually, they are multi-orgasmic."

Dianne: "Of course they have to bear children . . ."

Barb: "But then they get to bear children, they are the primary care-giver, the mom, the educator, the teacher of language and hygiene, and all the most important stuff."

Sam: "Well, men are able to lift things I can't. . ."

Vicky: "And they're good at opening doors and jars."

Sam was getting a little suspicious of where this was going and sought to interject a little distraction. She said, "I adore that a door can be ajar, don't you?"

That cracked everybody up.

Barb: "Well said. OK, Men do serve that purpose."

Dianne: "Don't forget about bug-killing."

Vicky: "And garbage remover."

Barb: "Yes, they are good at that as well."

Sam: "Don't bug me about bug killing. And if I can have babies I can probably take out the trash too. In fact I do."

Barb: "OK. . . so. You've basically taken it down to opening jars and lifting heavy things. I wouldn't disagree with you."

Sam: "Did you have a Father at home when you were growing up?"

Barb: "Well. actually my dad was a deadbeat and he skipped out when I was in grade school. Did you have a Dad?"

Sam: "Oh yeah. I still do. My parents are still together. I am actually closer with my Dad. My Mother is a very strong-willed person, a REAL bitch. My father is more laid back, takes things as they are."

Dianne: "Sounds like he would have to be."

Barb *(to Dianne)*: "Do you come from a strong Female family background, as I do?"

Dianne: "Hmm, well my mom is highly educated and very strong, but so is my dad."

Barb: "Are you an only child, as I am?"

Dianne: "Nope. I have one brother."

Barb (to Sam): "What about you, Sam?"

Sam: "Yep. I'm an only child."

Barb: "Do you consider yourself strong-willed and naturally dominant?"

Sam: "Yes, however I am not ready to take control

over anyone. For me things work in checks and balances; it's different for everyone."

Barb: "True, but you do consider yourself a Feminist first, right?"

Sam: "Yes, but I don't think females are superior. I don't think males are superior. We need each other."

Vicky, Dianne, Barb *(in unison, teasing)*: "Awwwwwe."

Sam: "Whatever works for each couple!"

Barb: "Understood."

In her diary that night Sam wrote: I am going to a restaurant and I am going to order the biggest burrito they have on the menu, and bring on this kid!

Nativity

The next trip to the hospital was the real thing. They had taken the advice in the old wives' tale about having a big Mexican food dinner and sure enough, the next day the birth was ON. Sam had her bags packed and it was a GO when the contractions started. The intake examinations began slowly, the nurse asking her questions, filling out forms, finding out how far apart the contractions were, telling her to relax. They got Sam into a gown and into a room. They hooked the monitors up to her stomach, to measure how close and regular the birth rhythm contractions were. Pretty soon they were certain that this was it—the baby was coming. Walker stood, bending over her, looking aware and intent at the side of her bed, holding her hand, looking into her panicked face and holding onto her tight when the contractions came.

She would clutch Walker's arm and contort her face in pain, clutching him tight, while he was in a panic—

trying to remember the Lamaze breathing. He, He, He. HAAAAA. . . He would be trying to sigh out the air, loud, trying to get her to synch her breathing up with his, but the contractions were so severe that she would double up and forget to breath at all!

The coaching nurse was on the other side of the bed and she tried to help get the Lamaze started too.

Breathe! Breath. He, He, He. HAAAAA. . .

Aahh!! Oooo!

"You just go ahead and howl all you want to, honey," the attending nurse said as she closed the door.

It was show time at the main focus on the high hospital bed, like they were participants at some kind of mass. The bed was the altar, and the host of acolytes were the white-robed attendants. Walker held her wrists in a strong but gentle grip. He got down into her face trying to pace her breathing but she would have none of it.

"I know we had a birth plan," the mother-to-be joked, "but it's changed. I just want drugs! I WANT DRUGS!"

There was no room for male power trip here, Walker thought. This is the realm of the female, I must go along. God this is it. I am trying to reach her but she is just so far away. She is going through all this pain, like a virgin being sacrificed at the life-altering initiation of motherhood.

Behind them, shadows came and went—people and the high priests and priestesses of life and science in white vestments hovering over the well from which new life was trying to burst onto the scene. They were looking up Sam's vagina with a bright flashlight. One of the robed acolytes got down there with a set of calipers to measure the progress of dilation. Walker felt like some dumb animal howling at the hole. Like Lamaze was some kind of strange incantatory language or ritual necessary to have the transubstantiation of matter into man occur.

"God, he's coming! Drugs! DRUGS. Bring me Drugs," moaned Sam.

Seeing her lying there, all hooked up to the machines, Walker had a kind of vision that she was held in some form of spider web and that they were being drawn in, falling through the tunnel. They kept the lights of the hospital room cool. The room is changing from being the high contrast of hard edged instruments connected to the soft woman. It's like stepping off into space. I'm the kind of person who does that—takes chances, makes huge leaps of faith—have done that all my life, but she isn't. The space was not some kind of special effects deal like out of a Frankenstein movie (though it might have been with the vital significance of the event) where there is electricity running up and down the outside of his wife's body traveling out into the machines, or anything like that. There was no big spark of lighting arcing across the towers of a Tesla coil zotting into the earth and heralding the vivification of the creature. I wasn't going to suddenly go wild and start shouting "It's alive!" when the new being was born. It was more like characters morphing, faces dissolving, time dilation and relativity. Who are the relatives that make up this extended family? It was family tree diagrams, fanning out and bending with the breeze in the shadows of the background, rising up and out through the ceiling and out of the building. And it was more like there were colors mixing, the mixing of races, going back and back through anthropology and archeology, back to the caves, to watching the archetypes—through the shadows they projected onto the cave walls. The trees of heredity go off in all directions, cross over and overlap, and these are people who have known each other in past lives.

For a moment Walker could feel the room dissolving in her screams of pain; something's coming in the relentless contractions, in the pull and push. An undulating water thing. It is flowing out to her, and pulling back, an undulating thing running through this human flesh. Pain was part of it too, pain undulating through his bride, pain undulating through their lives. At times she didn't know where she was or who she was.

In the middle of the night getting on toward morning the darkness turned into a kind of blueness with this tunnel vision. It is shuddering and undulating through, throwing up its wings every 3 to 4 minutes then subsiding. Sometimes it starts batting its wings faster and faster. Then subsides. A man feels out of place, shamed at what his biology has brought him to, they are probing into her well, legs open to the world, spelunkers of the ovarian trolley, for there is a hatchling kicking—trying to break off the last hold of the old and free itself to something new. Walker understood: This is someplace I definitely cannot go or cannot even know. He felt the light cone glowing around the now. It was like the monstrance, the life force showing itself.

Walker looked longingly at his wife's face, her lovely model's face with the high cheekbones, all sweaty now and freaked out. She looked lovely even so. A person was like a kind of menorah, a candelabra of lights, a tree of hereditary going back. Oh, we have the illusion that we are individuals with choice, but really love is the illusion that life creates so it will continue fanning out like a tree with its branches stretching their twig tips up into the collective unconscious, back and back into the genetic intelligence of the races, going back into the unfolding of the universe and the uphill struggle of order against entropy. Fiery trees. It was a picture of speeded up life passages, primogenitors before him, being born and leaping up and running, copulating, and dying all in a quick dance, going back—going back. It made him wonder what was it all for. It was all happening so fast whole lifetimes lived in an instant, so that you could see only the individual arc from birth to death left hanging in the air like a solar flare, a promontory coming out of the earth and going back before quickly vaporizing. So that you only saw this surface of holes, these turbulent sphincters, and beneath that something like a flame, the flame of life, a fire burning in the core of the planet, connected to the core of the universe, the flame looking for a way to leap out high before it came down and found another opening in which to return. And it filled his imagination with gratitude to have been given this vision. He was just a part of it all.

Walker tried to imagine the life force as some kind of ubiquitous Selector, ranging over all the dominant and recessive genes flowing down the river of bloodlines and flowing down from generations, swerving past traits. And this Selector was both within and without us; it has already been at work composing the genetic makeup of this new human being.

Trouble was, he knew the stories of only a couple of the closest branches, he could see only a couple of generations. He knew the story of his parents meeting in Montreal where his father was stationed a sailor during the war. And Sam's parents meeting on a cross-country train, her father a sailor too, during the war. His mother escaping from a large, close, family of Scots in the sticks of Ontario; her mother escaping a large Italian family from Chicago.

One tries not to feel like a pop-up in these moments,

a mutt born from fate. One might try astrology to understand the configuration of the moon and stars at the moment of birth to check out the gravitation influence. But why not try to understand it through some kind of biological potential influence, having to do with mind and physics? What if we could do some kind of reverse time travel, some kind of metempsychosis time travel. What is the now anyway. The now is a moving point in time, and around that point there is a cone opening up toward the future before it like a scoop funneling in the future. It is the collection of possibilities coming in from all directions. And coming off the back side of the now is another cone like a bow wave, in a mirror image of the forward looking cone. The now is at the intersection of two cones like positive and negative numbers going off in opposite directions from the zero of now—the backward looking cone being the force of what has happened in the past impacting others in the now and driving forward the future from the past.

Then this great big anesthesiologist came in. He was huge and had long round shoulders and a muscular build with long blond hair. He looked like Wild Bill Hickock or Kit Carson or General Custer with a long droopy handlebar moustache making him seem like he had just walked in out of the wild west, this tall cowboy, serious as a gunslinger, with the pockets of his jacket stuffed with syringes and vials of good drugs. Walker almost laughed out loud when he learned his name: Dr. Good. Walker fell into the whole western demeanor by saying to the anesthesiologist, in his southern accent, "Doc, she's really in a lot of pain. Can't you give her a shot of something really good. Quick."

"Oh, *Noooo*," said the anesthesiologist—drawing it out real slow and concerned, "we can't have that." He raised and lowered his eyebrows humorously and smiled a doper's conspiratory smile at Walker. "I've got something for that." And quick as a wink with a nod on the sly, he whipped out a shot and stuck it into Sam's backside.

To Sam the anesthesiologist was an angel of mercy holding his syringe aloft like a great sword about to come down on all the pain. And the angel said unto them: *Fear not! For, behold, I bring you good tidings of, if not great joy, at least no pain. And there ain't no better feeling than to stop hurting.* But what the anesthesiologist really did say was, "She ought not to be feeling any pain *now.*" To prove it, he raised her arm in the air, read a pulse, and dropping the arm, watched as the limb gracefully reposed itself back to her side.

And then things started going into slow motion, as Walker started to see the tunnel opening up to a vortex, as her face became a kind of landscape. For it was relaxing and for a moment the pain was subsiding, and in the contours of her face, her warm, flushed, dark Italian-Hungarian face he saw her own parents and tried to imagine their parents, going back to the remotest stories from her old father in the old country, in Hungary, about mining coal, and being a poor farmer by the side of the road when the archduke drove by in his big new European car, and that was the first time he had ever heard a radio. But beyond that, there were only the stories that still lived in the mind of that old man of natural medicines and beliefs, handed down from—yes, the Gypsies! Her people came from Gypsies, Romany back to the Mongol Huns. I'm married to a *gadje* girl. Could their lines have crossed before? What if it is true that they had been lovers in past lives. And then while the anesthesiologist was working real fast getting some tubes hung up and then starting a dripping epidural into his wife's back, Walker's imagination jumped across time and space to a medieval Gypsy wagon wandering across the Austria empire. She was a young, dark-haired Hungarian woman brought to this country as a mail order bride, with porcelain smooth skin—distractingly beautiful, eighteen with long black hair. She is lying in the back of the covered wagon giving birth, eyes lively wet, dark eyes staring, piercing, ahead, in the back of a small covered wagon carrying all their possessions across the Eurasian steppes, she is giving birth. Helpless. The Selector coursing and floating in the rivers of blood pumped through the veins of the people that have gone to make up you and me. Their stories, somehow imbedded, in the genetic memory? Metempsychosis time travel—only speeded up. See her face? It is dissolving. We've been coursing along, like flotsam on the river of life in flood, bursting its banks for months now. This is what forms the lines on a face. It has nothing to do with the sign at the moment of birth; that is just one force—gravity. We're floating, up-stream against the general downward turn of entropy—anti-entropy flowing up from my own childhood earliest memories: looking up at trees.

In birth the life force is an undulating water thing. Sometimes it moves and you just have to be riding in it—a boat floating along. It certainly helps to have the spinal. A shadowy manta ray thing where we are all being taken down, flowing through a tunnel. We are moving. We are holding each other in the night, and coming through this tunnel together in the birthing room. And she started flowing down the river. At first she is floating past him, she is lying in the bed as he is standing by the river, she is floating down the river, the lineage of these families going back, the merging of these family lines going back, it was like a river and she is a great sea otter on her back, floating back, dissolving, Ophelia floating back down the river and he is standing on the sidelines watching her go by.

They had met out on the Eurasian steppes. He had been one of the few warriors left after a battle with the Mongols and he had taken her into his hut, because a woman needs the protection of a warrior, and in the slaughter she had become separated from her family. And she knew they had loved each other before, and he knew it too. Walker thought, "I have loved you somewhere in a great forest."

He was a Celtic warrior and she a Hun's daughter. They met under a large oak tree at the crossroads in a clearing of the forest. There was a stele stone marking the miles to Auberge at the fork in the road. She had come to have her fortune told by the Celtic sorceresses. She would throw the rune stones and have them read. The girl fortune-teller, was sister to the big Celtic warrior-priest. He was taken by her dark beauty, the young woman and the dark man of the forests stood motionless in the light and the swirling smoke of the fire, their eyes met, and he knew he must posses this dark woman.

"I have loved you before in the old medieval forests of Europe," Walker almost said out loud.

Sedated, stoned as a mountain, the mother-to-be heard voices as if calling her from across a great divide. Something was happening with her baby.

Many hours had passed and she went in and out, and all the while the doctors had been, at least every half hour, coming in to prick the uncrowned baby's forehead and taking blood samples. These they carried across the hall for running oxygen percentage tests and bringing right back. After the oxygen content got below a certain level they called Sam and Walker into a quick consultation.

"We're going to have to do a Cesarean," said the doctor, "the baby's oxygen level in the blood is getting lower than we'd like. We do them all the time. There is very little danger, and you need to do it because somehow he is not getting a high enough oxygen concentration in his blood.

"Here, you must sign these consent forms."

Walker sighed them.

Working real fast, within a couple of minutes, they had the gurney spun around and accelerating down a hall of lights, the lights passing swiftly overhead, going by like full moons of passing months . . . he is moving along with her, the lineage of these families merging, family lines going back, it was *the* river, coming from the place where two forks of a river merged. And she was lying on that hospital bed under the round lights of the sun and floating swift down that river, and she saw her husband with her paddling their canoe down that river. She just lay back into the flow and let them have their way with her.

Romans with a villa, her father stationed in Jerusalem. He was a carpenter and she was the daughter of a Roman legionnaire. Her father hired him to do some work on their boat. They met at a cross roads, next to a stele stone. They had to step aside and watch a great column of soldiers pass.

"Look. There goes Caesar with his legions."

And because when two lines are joined, all the people who make up the nodes on the path are also joined. The baby has all that blood and presage flowing in its veins—(not to mention all the recapitulation of phylogeny). She was taking him over the rapids, the rhythms of motherhood, down the river, whether he wanted to go or not, into a place where the soul of this woman was still merged with the undifferentiated soul of her unborn child. Down the river of no return they plunged, where the nearing soul was waiting to merge with its new body.

As if he were a ghost—a person able to pass through walls—Walker, fearing for the life that was hers, saw it pass before him. He floated past some objects that were symbols of her former lives, guitar, song book, fisherman's net, a horse she had ridden to victory. Down the hall they were rushed, doors flying open, into a room—the operation theatre. A curtain was thrown open to reveal a large staff of doctors in white and nurses in green rapidly preparing. The operating room is filled with doctors and nurses and their mentors and teachers and arranged in tiers receding into the background were their parents and their parents . . . going back into time, attending the birth.

There was a curtain drawn across her middle so that they could not see the proceedings. He was close up to her face and she was holding his hand tightly, awake and aware. The new father glanced up and saw the swift movement of the surgeon's arm, saw the gleaming scalpel come down and saw only the movement of the arm, not the cut—he did not want to see the cut, which was abrupt and sure and over in an instant.

"Oh, my God, it feels so weird," was all Sam said.

But her eyes were wide with fear and amazement, and they pulled this little wriggling alien out of her, and there he was all wet and pocky and red and blotchy, and they carried him around to present him to her so she could get a quick look and then whisked him past over to a little table where they suctioned the mucus out of his nose, and he started breathing. As he went past Walker gave the freaked-out newborn a quick look, and the wrinkled little bug-eyed alien seemed to look right back at him as if he was already a punk rocker saying, "Whas'up Da." And the two were both shocked to see each other. Then they laid the baby all clean and swaddled in soft gauze, on his mother's breast. Shaved head, no teeth, all this spastic movement—a little junkie taken from his drip. A human expelled from the garden of paradise.

"Does he have all his fingers and toes," Sam asked, smiling, amazed.

Walker answered, "Yes. He's fine and normal. Thank God."

It was 3:13 in the morning; she had been in labor for eight hours. They sent him home where he crawled into his lonely bed. That night she awoke in the hospital with fitful machinations over who would keep an eye on the baby next to the nurses' station. There were some great nurses in there.

Walker returned to her the next day with some books for the three-day stay. "I thought you might like to clip these coupons. I know you like to clip coupons, so I brought the ones out of the paper." It was Thanksgiving, and Walker made a pecan pie for Sam and the staff. The pecans had been soaked in Southern Comfort, an old Texas recipe.

Here is the recently created father backing his car smartly down a narrow alley to the private exit at the back of the hospital. This exit is set up just for the joyous occasion when the new parents would walk out into the light of day with their tiny newborn human for the first time. Walker and Sam were like Joseph and Mary being thrust out of the garden of paradise—like Adam and Eve. Joseph and Mary had purchased the requisite, proper, government-required baby carrier seat.

Under the watchful eye of the matronly head nurse, Joseph tests the security of the car seat by yanking on it with a force equal to stopping the car at 43 mph in 20 feet.

The nurse—with a sobering look, as though she had the authority not to—hands off the new baby to Joseph, like a football pro doing the quarterback sneak. The new dad started running directions at the bottom of his attention. Consider the weight of the baby. Exactly how much force is needed to get the object from here to there. Consider its angle of repose and the receptacle toward which you are moving it. They should come with a manual, one that begins, "CONGRATULATIONS! You have just obtained one of this season's people." But they don't. Walker wonders how Joseph must have felt picking up the son of God. Be extra careful where ever you are carrying the baby, learn to pick your route carefully. Concentrate on doing nothing but carrying your young ward through space as though you were carrying a prince to a coronation (pomp and circumstance playing in the background) as you move stately and evenly through doors, and set him down gently in the back seat of the car to be strapped in.

How *will* you get your arms around him to dig him out of his car carrier when you get him home. Use slow force. Don't fumble, jerk or grab the baby. Let competent supportive fingers alight around your baby like the gentle parent you now are. Take him into your arms and be sure to support his neck as you don't want his head to fall off. When you pick up your kid up, you are picking up an extension of yourself. Handle your kid with consideration and they will smile at you.

And so the days pass. You are up and down so much in shifts that you shift from day phases into night phases and you get to study sleep deprivation. In a few months the new parents come to know it as the poor man's virtual reality. After a while Walker actually got into it. He thought of it as a discovery. It was like being in his own sleep lab. Where you are awakened several times in the night to face your dreams. He had always wanted to do research into lucid dreaming and somnambulistic peregrination.

God forbid that you should ever put him down with his eyes open. He will wake up screaming like something out of a horror movie with that high hue-ee whee wee sound track of violins being attacked in the background. He has to be carried with a smooth even motion. When Walker turns, or stops too quickly, or if he gets the baby's foot or his own foot caught in the bed clothes, as he is trying to get the baby into the bassinet, the little micro-hellion wakes up. A middle of the night change turns into bedlam because Walker has unceremoniously dumped the little bundle of joy back into the bassinet without making sure he was asleep. Another time Walker snatched and jerked him too fast out of the bath water and the banshee did begin to wail. Careful when you round a corner don't bump his head.

But you learn. Within a few days, the new father has perfected the art of "flying" the baby, which is lofting him through space along his most natural trajectory, the one with the least resistance.

They will teach you patience. They will force you to question habits of mind you have been carrying for years, because you thought that's just the way things are. Here is the new dad fumbling with the snaps of the undershirt. Here he has put the arms in first *before* putting the onesie on over the head—that is the way he dresses himself, that is the way he has always dressed. But more and more he has to learn new ways. In a way, the father has to become himself like a child, putting himself into the position of a child for whom all this is new. Remember, they are just trying out their new nervous system, they will gyrate and will jump out of your hands one way or just as easily bang their heads into your teeth the other. They will kick their legs when you are trying to put their pants on, and splay out their hands and clutch at the inside of the sleeve as you put a shirt on. Be careful the thumb does not get jammed. Babies come from the world where they don't clearly distinguish themselves from these objects. When you dress the baby pull the body of the tunic over the trunk first. Then put your hand down the sleeve, get a hold of his little hand like you were holding the petals of a flower from opening and gently pull it back up through the sleeve. Don't try to pull the sleeve up over the hand for they will inevitable splay the fingers out and catch up the sleeve in it. Don't get frustrated with all the snaps. They are much easier than buttons.

It was the cutest thing in the world when the proud parents took their new baby out in the stroller for the first time. Here are mom and pop teasing, arguing like brother and sister: "It's my turn to push the stroller."

"No it's my turn."

"Nuh, uh, it's my turn. You pushed it the last time."

Even the simple motion of sitting up, and tracking something with the eyes calls for a lot of motor and neural activity to be coordinated. Baby is able to do things over and over and over, because the rhythm is inherently good in toning and entraining their nervous systems. The baby with patience will practice the same thing over and over. As such the baby becomes like the guru of Joy.

Sleep Deprivation is the Poor Man's Virtual Reality

Domestic Multi-tasking for the Complete Mongol

Now here is the new dad giving the baby a bath. He is careful to get into the creases and folds of soft baby flesh where spilled and spewed milk and food accumulate to engender life of its own on man. In a fold under the right side of the neck is the place where the most milk spills and accumulates. Two manicured fingers take the wash cloth like a piece of dental floss, and slowly work it back and forth sliding the edge of the cloth through the folds cleaning out the guck.

Walker has learned how to fold laundry. He observes that sheets and blankets are surfaces that move in this space, and they have to be allowed to find their own lofting trajectory—then they fall just so.

There is a system for towels in the bathroom, where the towels are folded longways in thirds. This indicates they are neat and newly washed. When folded in half or not at all, then we know they are in process. Before the birth of his son, Walker had an utter disrespect for objects, and they got even with him— reaching out and barking his shins and getting in his way whenever possible. But not any more.

The weeks pass with the new dad trying to advance himself in his role. Trying to move up from being the grunt cook to becoming a secondary support person. He moves through the bathroom organizing and scrubbing, rinsing poop. Working his way up the ranks.

The Miracle of the Milk Expresser Machine makes it possible for the dad to occasionally become the source of nourishment for the screaming, squalling baby. It is so good to deftly boil the water in the microwave for exactly 3 minutes before deftly reaching into the refrigerator and there, almost glowing, like the Holy Grail, to find a bottle of mommy's milk—not that formula milk—sparkling in the refrigerator light.

Walker begins to see his wife as a marvel of organizational acumen. The baby's travel bag for example, organized into Primary and Secondary items. Primary items are: 1. Change of clothes (T-shirt, socks, outfit / hat) 2. Blanket 3. Paper + pencil 4. Plastic bags for dirty diapers 5. Toys 6. Paper towels 7. Wash cloth / burp rag 8. Cloth diaper. Secondary items are: 1. Pad 2. 2 diapers 3. Ziplock w/wipes or moist wash cloth 4. Q-tips 5. Pacifier 6. More Toys 7. Sweatshirt / hat.

Of course, Walker's dexterity is nothing compared to that of his wife. On their first outing to a restaurant, Walker and Sam are edified at how many things she can do with one hand. She can eat a whole seven course meal with a baby on her lap. It was amazing. He noticed how his wife, whenever she makes a move, seems to have calculated out the whole sequence of what is to be her *next* move. To grasp this level of centered mindfulness was like understanding the meaning to the great, ancient Zen koan about the sound of one hand clapping. For Walker, it was like a thunderclap of enlightenment. He realized women really do have a multitasking brain. But still, in spite of the limitations of his male, linear orientation, and a rather meager twisted-pair, donkey-trail connection between the feelings and the verbal speech area, (in contrast to the women's coaxial fiber-optic-bundle information-superhighway connecting the speech area to the emotions), Walker learns.

He starts thinking of her as "Dr. Mom". You know, like in that television commercial where the family is lined up outside the bathroom, and "Dr. Mom" is seeing her family-member patients one at a time and dispensing a nostrum. "Recommended by Dr. Mom." The family members are like lovable dependent patients waiting outside the doctor's office of a grade school in the hall. The guy, the husband, is really pathetic. He is depicted as a dufus who can't do anything for himself. Yes, Dr. Mom. She is an efficient machine. Whenever she makes a move she seems to have calculated out the whole sequence of what is next. And the next move after that.

Suddenly, Walker snapped to what was going on. In the year of our linearity, Anno Dominae 1992, Friday April 13th, in a red naugahyde booth of the Chacmol Mexican food restaurant, with this understanding of frames of time, he has discovered the simple and basic philosophy of ZIP/SNAP. (He named it that later in honor of the snaps on a baby's onesie). It is simply everything wants to move along the path of least resistance, everything is a geodesic in a curved space, zipping along a path of least resistance until it can snap into place. The new father has come to discover the simple and basic philosophy of ZIP/ SNAP. And the trajectory of zip is this minimal path trajectory. You can do everything you do with Zip. Keeping the condo clean, for example, is just a problem in ecology, and ergonomics, minimal paths to the objects, minimal effort to read the signs.

The new father becomes an assiduous student of the philosophy of ZIP/SNAP. One of the main aspects of this new philosophy is that it comes with an aesthetic of how to break down motion into its composites and recompose them in a more efficient way.

It is like an epiphany, once you get the understanding of an epiphany, you reach a higher plane, where you don't have to break these things down anymore; actually you are lucky to have the opportunity to break these movement and activities down. Suddenly, Walker knew that everything was going to go zip with his life right now. After you have been around for a while, you start to see the whole space and not just the path you are on through the space. And the trajectory of zip is this minimal path trajectory. Do everything you do with zip. Zip is an attitude.

Walker has come a long way since that gray day when wandering around the lonely condo he experienced that moment of shock where he was rudely jolted into the NOW by the realization he didn't even know where his wife kept her socks. He realized women live in present and future time, and he finds himself living more and more in other time or perhaps past time, or behind time. All his life he felt like a prisoner of time.

Walker started developing a computer program called *Feed the Baby*. The object of this program is to use the mouse to feed a working 3D baby character in the interface. You move the cursor, which is a life-size, bent-handled, silver spoon, past the shaking, weaving, bobbing head, past the clenched teeth, and when you release the mouse button, deposit some amount of substance in the baby's mouth. In the program he honors his wife with many interesting discussions, and he benefits from her observations. By tapping into her extensive knowledge, he builds a database with useful tips into the program along with budget and logistics. He fantasizes it will become quite popular. Walker thinks to make and sell video tapes based on the interactive training in the program. Then to take his gleaned insights and tapes onto the circuit of men's group meetings. They would be like toning and conditioning tapes for new parents.

Walker is ready to reveal the mysteries of Zip. The philosophy of Zip has shown him new signs in the constellations of his universe. He has moved beyond the old signs of Droid, Bimbo and Hypodermic Needle from his sad, prior, down-stud universe of life before marriage. The old signs were about fear and loathing and avoidance of exploitation in working man's blues. The new signs are Video Tape, Photon, Info. These are about memories and scrapbooks, attentiveness, communication and caring. About being prepared.

He imagines himself talking to a men's group on video tape:

Scene: Television Show. An interview format on a public access stage. Walker and interviewer in suits, sitting in comfortable chairs. A round end table with bottles of water between them. They are half facing each other and half facing an audience.

Narrator (VO): Tell lus about your new video tape..

Walker: Part of what is required to be in the Now, is to be able to let go of the past. If you can get up to the now, and you realize what a short duration the now is, then you will be able to see how things are discrete. Everything exists in its own time frame, its own time envelope, and you must catch it like it was the ring on the merry-go-round ride, or wait until its time comes around again.

It is simply that EVERYTHING wants to move along the path of least resistance, everything is a geodesic in a curved space, moving along a path of least resistance. Everything gives off its own light. It's a rainbow in curved air.

Domestic
Multitasking
for
the
COMPLETE
MONGOL

To Sam on her 43rd Birthday

A woman casts a sheet so that it lofts out over the
surface of a queen-sized bed.
A life pulls out of a dive intersecting another causing it
to veer off course.
An 8 lb. 12oz. baby is yanked out of a womb with
enough impulse to propel it into the world.
A man tests the security of a carseat by yanking on it
with a force equal to stopping the car at 43 mph in 20
feet.
The timer on a microwave is set to beep in 1 minute.
A woman in sneakers pushes a stroller due west over a
sidewalk at 43 ft/min.
A toddler pushes a toy choo-choo train northeast across
carpet at 43 ft/min.
A woman singing in counterpoint holds a note 2 octaves
higher than middle C.

A woman swings a bat with enough force to drive a

softball left of center 43 yards.
A woman on a phone tries to listen between two sirens,
one her toddler wailing an octave lower and 4.3 decibels
louder than the police car siren outside on the street.
One glance from a parent sends a message at the speed
of light to the other parent.
A perfect parking place, minimal distance between the
market and the drugstore and the bank, lying at the
centroid of a polygon of streets intersecting those places,
is found by a woman praying to a parking goddess
named Gladys.
A woman looks out her east facing kitchen sink window
and raises her eyes 43° to the moon and other quasi-
stellar objects and wonders if the heavenly bodies float
in a sea of gravity.
A woman blows bubbles with an initial velocity at the
hoop of 43 ft/sec. Three of them float to the surface of
the bath and stick together so that the smallest possible
surface which will contain the three quantities of air and
keep them separate is maintained.
A 30 lb. toddler with an 8 inch reach, strikes down with
full force the surface of his bath water with both hands
open.

In what direction
do the bubbles
falling
through warm air
toward the surface
of the water
float?

The Tabernacle of Dr. Mom

Sometimes all this domesticity and service got to driving Walker crazy. It brought up a lot of psychological stuff for him. He was starting to have these projections of his mother on his wife. He started writing a kind of "bookmovie": *The Tabernacle of Dr. Mom.* It was supposed to be about him going back in time being watched over by his own parents. His own mom. It was about Projection. And it was about feeling more for his own kid, who he gave the nickname Shredder, because he was such an energetic and confident little micro-hellion.

The first scene came to Walker as he was standing in the bathroom brushing his teeth and wondering where he had learned to do that. Being a parent made you feel what it was like to be a helpless kid. It allowed one to look at himself from outside himself, as if he was a kid.

Dr. Mom has an almost pathological horror and fascination with the mouth.

Scene: Grade school child in a big asphalt school yard addressing camera

Child: Dr. Mom taught us how to insert a small bundle of hog hairs coated with a magic cream or powder into the mouth, and by moving the bundle in a highly ritualized sequence of gestures,

(child pantomimes brushing teeth)

in a mostly up and down motion,
rather than side to side,

(child illustrates)

we satisfied her penchant for oral hygiene.

It must all seem so weird to the infant. Walker wanted to try and feel more of what little Shredder was going through. It was his job in life to take care of little critter. So it was in the spirit of trying to look at the world with the strange awareness of a linoleum lizard that he wrote *The Tabernacle of Dr. Mom.* It was kind of a tour of Dr. Mom's dream house. You know, that Dr. Mom from the TV commercial, the one who is dispensing nostrums to the family. But this was a sequel to it—they get the same spokeswoman to act in it. We are taken on a tour of her dream house. And we start to find out what she is really like.

THE EYES OF DR. MOM

Scene: Sparkling all modern kitchen. Formica, tile, and stainless steel. The kitchen is sleek and modern. The floors are buffed shining burnished sunset Apache flash tile. The countertops are of a deep obsidian black marble that you could get lost in. A stainless steel refrigerator is built-in to one wall and a matching stainless steel range with a stainless steel hood is across the room from it. Everything is staggeringly bright. There are two large windows, one in the north wall and the other in the east. There is also reset track lighting. Multiple glass cupboards and cabinets reflect more light. The flatware is stoneware with somber Grecian motif. A stainless steel door is open to a stainless steel pantry.

Narrator (*Voice Over, enthusiast*): This is the *office* of Dr. Mom.

Scene: Dr. Mom, the little old frowzy lady, with an apron and white hair and big fifties-style glasses dangling from a chain is taking us on a tour, indicating areas with a sweeping gesture of the hand.

Dr. Mom: I've designed the perfect house with the kitchen at the center and all the rooms distributed around it. Everything is in white. The rooms are back-lit so everything is seen in high contrast, in relief. The white is to spot any bugs or bacteria or cobwebs, so they can be immediately TAKEN OUT!

Scene: Blueprint from above. The rooms of the house are arranged around a central kitchen. There is a line of sight from the kitchen to every room in the rest of the house.

Narrator (VO): The center of the hub was the kitchen/ dining room.

Dr. Mom: The space was highly organized into little sub-spaces.

Narrator (VO): She was the center of the nest, and it was her function to forge the mettle of her children in the furnace of that kitchen, to mold them into malleable beings.

Dr. Mom: The rooms have a view out to the world and a doorway back into the kitchen, into the center of the domain of Dr. Mom. Into every one of the rooms, the eyes of Dr. Mom could peer.

Narrator (VO): But there was no connection between the rooms, so their inhabitants didn't really get to know each *other*. They could meet around the dinner table and get to know each other there under the watchful eyes of Dr. Mom. Divide and conquer, sections of a pie. The house an efficient working machine, connected "cells" of an automata. The layout of the house is actually only the topology of any house, distributed in a way to maximize the efficiency of Dr. Mom by reducing the effort needed to observe the others in the house.

Sometimes the Father, Mr. Mom, was allowed into the kitchen. He is sort of a support figure, a guardian, too, a preferee among Dr. Mom's underlings.

In fact, he was necessary. Dr. Mom in a brilliant stroke, had the kitchen arranged like in a modern house, where the halls appeared to go off into private rooms, but really the rooms were watched by a careful arrangement of mirrors and windows. This was done so that the individuals in the rooms could not see into the domain of Dr. Mom, yet knew they were being observed. Or they could possibly be being observed, and naturally had to assume that fact, so this allowed the nuclear family in a standard house with only two guardians to create a very effective system of surveillance.

Of course, this system was elaborated upon and made more efficient later in schools, where each room contained a number of individuals kept from getting to know each other by aisles and rows.

DR. MOM OF THE WITHERING LOOK

Dr. Mom was master of the withering look. I mean if you looked at her dream house from above, though it looked like a regular house, in fact an ideal sweet suburban house with a lawn and sidewalk and rows of bikes and toys parked in perfectly neat angles along the side of the sidewalk as you walked up to the front door, it was an essentially circular house. Mom was at the center of things and everything else was arranged in circles around her. Depending on who was closer or further away from the center, the hierarchy of distance was classified, qualified, measured, compared and differentiated, and then judged. The eye of home. Expanded out into the world. But even more, the eye of Dr. Mom became so much a part of the individual's psyche, it provided the basis of what was understood as normal.

Dr. Mom had her cookies to give out: she spun dependencies like strands of thread into a fabric of time, of activity, of behavior, of speech, of the body of sexuality. In short, it became the Unconscious. The eyes of Dr. Mom have an outpost inside your own head.

I mean there were times when you could triangulate the situation with your siblings shift the focus on to them, have them soak up some of the disappointment—thank god there were those. You could form various coalitions, insist on some small aspect—haircut or clothes, sometimes dictate even what school to go to—but these were minor recapitulational feints in the long duel for the dominance of your soul.

Each head became an outpost with the guardian's gaze now upon the individual from within.

DR. MOM AND THE MICROCOSM

She worried about ants swirling around in their little black dens. And a swirling pestilence of microbes warring unseen in the intestines, the whole microbial world out there, behind the whiteness of the baseboard.

She was constantly at war with dirt. Dr. Mom really believed in cleaning. She was always cleaning and organizing and straightening up. Always a force of anti-entropy, the microbe was her enemy. She thought they conspired and carried out campaigns against her. The world outside was, for her, this endless tide of filth which had to be halted at her door. She was the guardian against these forces of chaos and ooze that had to be stopped, moreover eradicated, wiped out.

THE TABERNACLE OF DR. MOM

Scene: White tile bathroom, with sparkling plumbing fixtures gleaming. A mirrored medicine chest reflecting. Toothbrushes all in a row.

Narrator (VO): Here we are in the bathroom shrine of Dr. Mom. We have an altar made of porcelain through which water flows. It is embedded in a mirror covered wall that is a surface in which a person can see himself. And above that altar, is the tabernacle of Dr. Mom. The tabernacle of Dr. Mom is the medicine chest built into the wall.

Dr. Mom: In here, Dr. Mom keeps many of the charms and magical potions without which no one in the family would be able to live. From this most hidden inner sanctum, Dr. Mom dispenses these magical charms.

Narrator (VO): If the outer life is spent in economic pursuits, it is here in the bathroom that the inner life — the pursuit of good healthy appearance occurs.

Dr. Mom is a channel of our culture's body ethos: the human body is ugly and its natural tendency is toward debility and disease.

CUT TO:

Scene: Zoom into close-up of Dr. Mom. She has an enigmatic, all-knowing, Mona Lisa smile, and her picture is set into the famous painting.

Narrator (VO): In the dream house of Dr. Mom, there are several of these bathroom shrines.

Scene: White tiled bathroom with many hoses and nozzles that spray various torrents and mists. It looks like a huge 3D Rube Goldberg contraption. Dr. Mom is conducting the tour.

Dr. Mom: They would all be tiled, and there would be these hoses and brushes on mechanical arms that hose and scrubbed down everything in the room. Then these other arms would come out of the walls and squeegee everything down into a stainless steel drain.

CUT TO:

Scene: Women sitting on a bench in a park. They have their kids with them.

Narrator (VO): In fact when the Moms get together they often find out how many bathroom shrines they have in a house. It is a measure of wealth.

CUT TO:

Scene: Extremely well appointed, opulent bathroom, of Donald Trump, surfaces of gold etc.

Narrator (VO): The bathroom shrines of the wealthiest are walled in marble, trimmed in gold and porcelain.

CUT TO:

Scene: Small, standard American tract housing bathroom.

Narrator (VO): The poorer families imitate the rich with tiles applied to the walls, plumbing of chrome plating, and tubs of burnished fiberglass.

While each family has at least one such shrine, the rituals associated with it are not family ceremonious but are private and secret. The rites are normally only discussed with children, and then only during their formation period when they are being initiated into these mysteries.

The charms and magical potions of Dr. Mom in the tabernacle are many and without them no one in the family would be able to live.

The preparations are bought from a variety of pharmacists. These pharmacists are given money. They are the only ones who can read the ancient and secret language of the doctors who also have to be rewarded heavily for bestowing these magic gifts.

These valuable prescriptions and charms are not disposed of after use, but are put in the tabernacle of the household shrine.

With time, no one could remember all the ills imagined and real upon which they are supposed to effect cures. That is how they begin to take on magical properties, just by their presence in the tabernacle, they ward off disease. Of course, for magic to work you must be a worshiper. A worshiper of—you guessed it—Dr. Mom.

THE SKINNERIAN BABY'S CHANGING TABLE

Scene: Dr. Mom smiles.

Dr. Mom: Cleanliness is next go godliness. Won't you have a look at my new developments? It's called the Skinnerian baby's changing table.

Scene: A high-tech Skinnerian baby's changing table

Narrator (VO): The neonate social unit wears velcro clothes that rip away.

He is moved on a conveyer through a little box called a Skinnerian box in which little hoses force water into cracks, just like the way cars are painted by painters on the assembly line. Put the baby in one end and he is stripped, hosed down, squeegeed off, slipped into new pampers, and comes out the other end of the black box.

The Tabernacle of Dr. Mom

Father Night

Scene: Bedroom in the dark. Chest of drawers. Mirror. Bed with man and woman in it, their heads on pillow above covers. It is deep night. Suddenly the sound of loud rap or reggae music outside. We hear Walker's internal monologue in Voice Over, in his own voice. He is waking up.

Walker*(Voice Over (internal monologue))*: This all started when I was woken up in the middle of the night by some guy outside playing a Boom Box. Jungle tom-toms serenading the whole neighborhood! *Gahhha*! The natives must be restless tonight.

Baby *(Voice Over)*: WWhhAAAAAAAAA!!

Walker (VO): And ***my*** little native, is woken up too.

Walker (*to his wife in bed*): I'll take care of it.

Scene: Walker gets out of bed and heads groggily out into the baby's room. Checks baby. Checks the blinds, to peek outside. We see his face in profile looking through a slit in the blinds. Sound of rap music outside louder.

Walker (VO): And I thought, I'll just go over to the window . . . and slide the blinds back a little bit. Just a little bit, because the music is really loud . . . and I don't know what kind of guy I'm dealing with.

Scene: View outside second story window down to the corner three houses away. It has been raining and the streets are glistening. A person dressed in what looks like a large pile of leaves is shambling along. He goes into the center of the intersection, where there is the most light, and stops. He is a very large black man with a cowboy pimp hat and shades, wearing what appears to be a large overcoat all mounded up with ribbons or fringe. It is a moving avalanche of rags and other objects—festooned with embroidered epaulets, adorned with medals and ribbons, plus various badges, miscellaneous braid and other ornaments all over what appears to be a black and orange biohazard jump suit. He is holding a giant black boom box on his shoulder up near his ear and listening intently to LOUD reggae music. His hand is draped over the top of the boom box, holding it in the crook of his arm.

Walker (VO): A guy like that would be so OBLIVIOUS, he could be capable of ANYTHING. And I just peek through the blinds because I don't want to attract the fucker over here or anything.

Scene: We zoom in closer onto the street person. On the head of the street-person is an incredible pile of snarled dreadlocks under a great big superfly hat. He is doing a shambling dance and sway to the reggae music, as he allows himself to be led by the sound; it pulls him first left, then right, doubles him back on himself, spins him around, drawing him deeper and deeper into the reggae groove. We can just barely hear him mumbling, moaning, scat singing, chanting—sometimes loud, sometimes soft—nodding to the music. A car approaches making the wet landscape glimmer. Like a bull-fighter, the street person yields very little ground to the advancing car.

Walker (VO): I like to brood and think and prowl around in the night myself. But this is outrageous! He is boogying on the street!

CUT TO:

Scene: We are looking from the point of view of the street person, back up at the window where Walker is. The camera zooms up to the window and we see the face of Walker looking out.

CUT TO:

Scene: Back inside bedroom, Walker pulls back from the window, we see a shocked, disconcerted look on his face.

Walker (VO): O, No! It's the Boogeyman! *(Walker places his palm on his breast, dismayed)* I'm a new father, and I haven't even got used to it yet. I mean, it's been bringing up a lot for me.

Baby *(Voice Over)*: ! WWhhAAAAAAAAA!!

Scene: Walker moves away from the blinds, walks across the room to the crib. Zoom to his big hands start to lift tiny baby out of crib bed. The baby has a little knit cap on. Big hand under baby's head. Baby's whole body lying along the man's arm. Other hand on baby's front. Baby being lifted out of bed. Sound of rap music outside. Digital clock shows 3:13.

Walker *(Voice Over (internal monologue))*: I wonder what it is like to look at the man from the Child's Point of View.

FADE TO:

Scene: A lot of this shot from a child's POV, things rushing past. The world of Giants. Garish, through blurry eyes, bleepy. Like we are inside something, a submarine and it is moving. Close up of father from fish eye lens.

FADE TO:

Scene: Walker carrying baby through the house.

Walker (VO): So I pick the little one up and head downstairs to heat up his bottle. I'm carrying him in kind of like a football hold. Where you hold the baby's head in the palm of your hand, and they just rest there along your arm.

And it was a warm night. And it's not unpleasant music. But I'm scared. It's 3:13 AM, and there's some guy outside playing a boom box, and he must be moving, by the way the sound is dopplershifting around.

Scene: Seen from behind, as father, holding baby aside, looks through a chink in the blinds again. Zoom down to the glistening street and the moving man.

Walker (VO): There he is on the corner, about three houses away, standing there with his boom box swinging it around!?

I fear him. I hate him, his inconsiderateness, his complete obviousness.

And then I started to try and pity him. He was obviously a homeless avatar off his meds; probably spent more nights outside than a cave man and was hardened off against it.

Best not judge . . . he that is without sin throw the first stone.

FADE TO:

Scene: What Walker sees what he is saying in the following:

Walker (VO): But his vibe, the way he was attuned to the music. It is almost like the rags were a kind of seaweed that came waving out off of him as he twirled, like fingers on a hand waving, beckoning, pointing in some strange dark madness-kingdom cartoon. The way the feathers and rags and scarves flew up off his clothes when he danced.

Scene: To see what Walker imagines, we see the street person as underwater so all the fringe floats out. Or in a slow motion movie with the movement of the costume parts flying out in time to the movement and the music.

Walker (VO): I'm probably the only person who would see this. His vestments were like prayer flags on a mountain in a great spiritual wind, some kind of caring medium of which the wind was the prayer carrying instrumentality.

CUT TO:

Scene: Long shot of Walker from behind as he begins swaying to the rap music outside; lifts arm, holds baby as if the baby were the boom box.

Walker *(sings along with the distant boom box music)*:

Du duwapa du duwapa BO, UUOO SHAN

Scene: Walker is holding the baby in one hand, the baby's head in the palm of his hand and the baby's body lying draped with his back along Walker's arm. Baby and Father are regarding each other.

CUT TO:

Change in POV to be from a frightening baby's view of the Father, through fish eye lens into the worlds of giants. Shadowy.

CUT TO:

Change POV back to Walker holding 'Boom-box' baby.

Walker (VO): They are so dependent on us.

If Sam saw me holding him like this, she'd give me hell.

Scene: Still holding baby, Walker looks out window again.

Walker (VO): And I can hear the music moving like a train going by, and I can see him, the Boogeyman, moving. And he's a big dark guy, and he's dressed up in rags, like a mummy! Or a Gypsy or something. *(pause)* Now he turns it down for a passing car.

Scene: Carries baby downstairs in low light. Black and White shifts into color, which comes and goes with the intensity of light. Shadows of trees projected through big window over the stair well, moving, creepy, as he carries the baby downstairs.

Walker *(singing along with the distant boom box music)*:

Du duwapa du duwapa BO, UUOO SHAN

Walker (VO): Sleep deprivation is a poor man's virtual reality. Now what would be a nice scholastic word for dream travel.

Scene: Walker's face, wrinkled brow, thinking hard.

Walker (VO): Oneirodisplaysia!! Wow! Dream travel, or what is displayed on the mind's eye when traveling in dream reality. Oneirodisplaysia! Now there's a word and a world to stumble on into at 3:13 in the morning.

Scene: Walker seen from behind, Father holds baby close to him in a hug, while he looks out drapes again. View outside of condo garden, a little swinging gate, with carriage light on top of it. We see through a window in the garden wall beyond to the street. The window has bars being used as a trellis for a vine to climb. We are looking through the leaves of trees swaying in the breeze almost in time with the rags and ornamental ribbons on the Boogeyman's overcoat—moving and swaying in time. Reggae sound is louder, closer.

Walker (VO): Now it's back up. Gaahh! Now he is pointing the Boom Box toward the building! I wonder if he has learned the ancient sound attack techniques they used against the walls of Jericho, trying to vibrate them down.

Scene: Walker seen from behind as he holds the baby close to him, while peering through drapes out down-stairs glass patio door.

Walker (VO): Somebody just yelled at him and ran him off.

(quickly backs away from the window)

He got into an argument with them!

He stomped off toward ***our*** side of the street.

(Slowly with fear)

Then I just start slipping into this *old fear* of the night. I wonder if this *GUY* is going to try and come over here or something.

Then I start thinking about calling the cops.

But they probably have a breathalyzer over the phone. . . Then I start to worrying about my parking tickets. I wonder if they are all paid up. I don't trust cops.

Scene: Walker holds the baby while he peers around the edge of the drapes. The Boogeyman is standing in the exact center of the intersection. Looks up at the street light. He twirls around like the intersection is a stage or an altar, moving in and out of the spot light.

Walker (VO): Now he's back in the center of the intersection.

He's taking back the street. He's definitely taking space! Dancing with the boom box at the center of the intersection!

Walker *(sings along with the distant boom box music)*: BO, UUOO SHAN

Walker (VO): He's got a nice deep, choir voice this street dancer, and he's singing along with the boom box late at night. He likes the echo in it. It is a kind of reggae chant. I wonder how anyone can be so oblivious! Guy like that is probably so far gone. . .

There he is, cradling a boom box in his arms and dancing with it at 3:13 in the morning.

I look out there. Now he's leaning against the wall admiring the arrangement of the street lamp.

Scene: Father's reaction, from behind—shakes head in disbelief. He walks across small living room to kitchenette. On formica counter is a baby padded carrier seat.

Walker (VO): It is like that great spot light that he always wanted to step into.

Scene: Walker places the baby carefully in carrier. Places the little blue, yellow, and pink Magic Bear stuffed toy into the kid's hands. Snaps down shoulder harness. Turns carrier so that baby can watch the father work in the kitchen.

Walker *(speaking directly to baby)*: There must be something in the air tonight.

Walker (VO): People are afraid to call the cops.

Note: The following dialogs occur while we watch the Father deftly prepare the bottle. He opens the doors to the refrigerator, and we see inside an aura around the stubby bottle of baby's milk with nipple covered under a little plastic shell; he takes out the baby bottle, and he closes the door . He reaches up into the top cabinet and opens it, and he takes out a rather large cup. He reaches over and turns on the water at the sink; he fills the cup up with water, and he turns off the tap. He moves over in front of the microwave; he presses a large square button and the door swings open, and he has to stop it from bouncing closed. He gets the large cup of water and places it inside the vault of the microwave. It looks like the set of a stage in there. He closes the door with a loud ca-THUNK that startles the baby. As he keys in the number 3 : 0 0 and presses START, there is a beep with each keystroke. The microwave whirs to life.

Scene: Walker opens refrigerator door. We see inside past him an aura around the stubby bottle of baby's milk. Gets baby bottle of milk out of fridge.

Walker: *(looking over shoulder, speaking directly to baby)*: It's old Father Night.

(Scene: Sets bottle of milk on counter.)

Walker (VO): Yep. It starts to come back to me now.

I'm reminded of something from childhood. An older car, it must have had a running board, this was in the 50s in Montreal, and I'm sure there were still plenty of them around. It skidded around a corner. And my mother said:

FADE TO:

Scene: Bright 40s kitchen, view from behind of young woman in an apron standing at sink. She is looking out the curtained window; the curtains are blue gingham gently moving in the breeze of the open window. She has long hair swept up the style of the 40s.

Mother's voice (in VO): *(exaggerate mother's voice, she is imprinting fears)* "Look it's being chased by police. They are gangsters!"

WIPE TO:

Scene: Walker standing at sink, in the same relative position as the mother in the previous scene. He is running water into cup.

Walker (VO): And I began, in a child's mind, to associate this, this unknown chaos outside the window of home, going on in the dark, with badness. In a child's mind, they were part of Father Night—these gangsters in the vast frontier of night-space beyond the light of home.

(Looking thoughtful)

I begin wondering about why this is connected. . .in my mind: the car being chased by police. . . in my mind, and . . . gangsters and . . . the night.

(Realizing)

It was a direct communication of a mother's fear. My mother said with authority:

FADE TO:

Scene: Young woman in 40s kitchen, leaning over to speak.

Mother's voice (VO, (*whispering a scary story*)): "They are members of a gang."

FADE BACK TO:

Scene: Walker in kitchenette as he turns from sink and carries cup with water to microwave.

Walker (VO): Mommy's milk. Must not microwave that. Has the good antibodies in it.

(mumbling more memories)

I think the gangsters were shooting back. Yes! It was a running gun battle with police! I think they had tommy guns in the GANGSTER'S car. They might have been hanging on the running boards!

It was a warm summery night like this one.

(Puts cup of water in microwave)

The black leather jacketed gangs, with their loud motorcycles—the GANGSTERS—could be anywhere, like they were invisible, part of the night itself.

Scene: Inside microwave walls look like they are wall-papered. Like it is a room.

Walker (VO): They could get you, and take you out into the country, to the end of a long dark road and inside a dark house, down the hall and inside a room within a room, put you in a closet in that room. And do anything they wanted to you.

Somehow I associated this fear of the night with my father and with motorcycle gangs.

Scene: Closes door with ka-thunk. This startles the baby. Walker looks at baby; talks to baby in carrier seat

Walker *(directly to baby)*: Did your father scare you? Are you afraid of Father Night, too?

Scene: At the microwave. Man's hand types in numbers on the keypad. With each finger stroke, an orange number appears on the little digital display accompanied by a beep. Finger presses Start. Microwave starts, makes a loud whirring machine noise.

Walker (VO): I used to wake up in the middle of the night all sweaty like you are now, and think that the motorcycle men led by Marlon Brando are going to come in and get me.

(The following sounds are made like cooing as Father is looking closely into baby's face, talking, to baby in carrier.)

Walker: Brrrmmm brrmmmm. Brrrmmm brrmmmm. BRRRMMM BRRRMMM! BRRRMMM BRRRMMM!

I'll tell you about *Father Night.*
Father Night is the shadow side of my own self, and it is something you will have to come to know of me and will some day have to know of yourself. We all live in a time line from Eros to Thantos. Perpetuating adolescence is trying to hold onto Eros and push Thantos farther off. Father Night coming to get me. Becoming a father reminds me of that.

Scene: Walker looks at the baby, reaches out his free hand starts playing with the shadows on the wall;

moving hand in front of lamp; baby and man looking at shadow play.

Walker: Father Night is this shadow that hangs over all men. So how do I show him to you?

If we're going after the shadow . . .

(Pause. Looks down at his own shadow then up toward the light)

We've got to look toward the light, the source of the shadow.

After the light . . the sun around which your mind orbits *(pause)* is made up of the father and the mother.

The way I thought of it was like a triangle, your father on one side and *(pause)* your mother on the other *(pause)* and where the two come together—that's you.

Scene: Smiles at the infant, points finger, slowly lowers it to touch delighted baby on the chest.

And where the two come together—that's you.

Walker: *(talking directly to baby in carrier)* It goes back to this basic triangle. Your mind is made up of these polarities, the mother and the father; and they keep getting switched around. Father Mother, Male Female.

Walker (VO, *indicting internal monologue): But* if the mother is not something that you want to hold up as a mental model, hold up the mother's brother, your maternal uncle. At least in my case I took after this uncle and not my father.

Scene: Orange numbers of microwave digital display counting down backwards.

Walker: My father and my uncle. . . . These are two men my mother loved. . .OK? So I'm trying to get inside my family tree. That great structure that is between you and the sky. Who is Father Night?

Scene: Camera slowly zooms into the window on the microwave door. We are looking through a window and see a classroom. We zoom in the classroom where a projector is projecting a movie onto a screen. We are looking at an old time black and white movie.

Walker (VO): You have to run this world backward to see who Father Night is. Father night is time, is entropy.

Scene: The black and while movie projected on the screen is a documentary. Walker's voice becomes the voice over narrator of the documentary assuming a 'professional' style voice. The camera quickly pulls back to show that we are looking through the microwave window, able to see the numbers in the display count down backwards.

Walker (VO, *in professional documentary voice*): It would be as though, suddenly the paint were slurked off the boards of these walls of the houses. They would stand there bare for a minute. Then the boards would start coming off very fast . . . time elapsed . . . board by board. Like the ivory keys in a piano, they fly across the space and insert themselves into the backs of trucks! Like cards being dealt at a great game.

Soon there is only the frame of the houses left. Then they start to come apart from top down: leaving vacant lots.

The wood in the boards is yearning, longing to be back in the wild again. And they DO get back into the wild.

We see trucks backing up at break neck speed, back to the saw mills, where the boards leap off the trucks into the mill, run along rollers onto the whirling, circular saw blades which weave and mend the boards together into logs again, until the logs leave out the front of the mill whole, round and barky, where the whole logs leap back onto bigger trucks and race backwards into the woods, where they roll off the trucks and roll back up the hill and stand themselves up majestically—peaceful, looking over all.

Scene: Documentary style, Walker is standing under a giant Douglas fir. Its trunk shoots up two stories before sprouting any branches. We see from beneath it into a starry night sky opening through branches. The camera moves up and we are looking along the boughs as the night twinkles beyond.

Walker (*Voice Over track inside of documentary*): It's like Father Night is this huge strong nurturing tree we all want to get back to, get back inside of, this sacred tree that was between you here on the earth and the energy in the . . . sky.

Everything in this whole world yearns to be free.

Like a carpenter working in wood, I'm exposing the grain of my family tree. You have to construct your own character out of the composite of your mother and father.

Look at what has become of all that wood.

Scene: Camera pulls back, we see beyond the tree in the distance endless housing sprawl crawling over the hills (little boxes on the hillside).

Walker *(talking directly to baby in carrier):* Carpenters are the happiest people—physical, making good joinery. Surfaces filled—going off at right angles.

Worked in wood. They like to feel the strength in the wood.   See how the trees are beings that climb hills, climb toward the light, put down roots to hold back the entropy, to fix the free energy. They have a strategy of survival. The would: (*spells it out)* W_O_U_L_D.

Scene: While the following, CUT back and forth between male weight lifting contest and forest boughs.

Walker (Voice *Over track inside of documentary):* Strong muscular creatures, showing off their torsos and upper body, in various poses, their limbs flexed leaning into the hills. This sacred tree between you here on the earth and the energy in the sky.

Scene: Walker picks up baby from carrier and holds him, talking directly to him.

Walker: Will you love me? Will I love You?

Father (VO): Now I'm a Father, and I see Father Night as this male energy who is the consort of Mother Earth.

(*Takes cup of hot water out of microwave)*

Father Night is the one that makes the turn of the circle, of the cycle in to the next generation. Death is the

Father of Life. Father Night is Death, Father Night is the shadow of god.

Scene: Puts bottle into cup of hot water. He turns toward the baby again, and snaps back from reverie. Announces to baby:

Walker: And I had an uncle. Roddy MacDougall, Here today I'm caught up in him.
(Leans down as if he is getting the question from the baby)

Why . . . is . . . he . . . here . . . in . . . me?

He is the great father. That I am always looking for.

He pulls me up. That kind of buoyancy, great male energy, enthusiasm, anything is possible.
(Leans down again as if to get question from the baby:)

What . . . is . . . his . . . secret?

Love! A kindly agape´. A generous hopeful enthusiasm.

He is the big brother watching from the side. Protecting the little ones from falling and hurting themselves. Where did he get that? And can I get some?

Scene: Inflates, expands chest, like a good big uncle. Takes the bottle out of the cup of warm water.

Walker *(VO (internal monologue))*: He was always a bachelor when I was coming up, he didn't get married until late in life. Like me. In fact, he was 42 when he got married, and I was 42 when I got married. Like some kind of transgenerational threshold got fulfilled at last to free me up.

Walker *(talking directly to baby in carrier)*: My father, on the other hand, graduated from college, was a research chemist, was married and a father by 22. He met my mother while serving on a Navy ship during the war.

Scene: Walker gets a dish towel that is folded over a rack near sink and dries off bottle. Walker starts dancing around the kitchen with the bottle held out at arm's length.

Walker *(talking directly to baby in his carrier)*: He was an excellent dancer. I remember being shocked watching him and my mother jitterbug in the kitchen. He would roll her over his shoulders and pull her between his legs, throw her high up in the air, and she would come down, and she'd catch him with her legs squeezing him around the waist with her legs, then he would bend over and dip her down to the ground, making her legs go point up high into the air, to the ceiling.

Walker (VO): But even more than dancing, I think he liked drinking and hanging out with his buddies—shooting pool. My streetwise father and my innocent uncle both were in the war.
(pause)

We were immigrants, without any relatives. I was always the New Kid in school. We moved around a lot. I was always the New Kid on the block.

I have to admire my father for having the courage to pluck up his family and move to another country.

Scene: Checks the temperature of milk on back of wrist

as he is getting ready to give it to the baby. Talks to the baby.

Walker: Got to make sure it's not too hot.

Walker (VO): You know, this is a really advanced design. The bag is better than the bottle. But it would be hard to tell that to the connoisseur. Yes, tell the maitre de the finest wine comes in a plastic liner with a nipple.

Air is the enemy of wine. Though I'm sure a friend of the grape.

Scene: (fits bottle to the mouth of the baby.)

Walker *(talking directly to baby in his carrier)*: Here's your bottle.

Scene: Walker smiling and watching baby.

Walker (VO): My father really liked his bottle, too. My father gradually slipped into alcoholism. I used to blame myself for being such a burden. But I realize he had just lost his way. It's easy to do, done it myself often.

I don't know how on earth he managed it, but he drank at least a fifth of whisky along with a couple of 6 packs—every day! And still managed to never miss a day of work. He had the constitution of a pit bull. You've got to admire that.

(The following is said in a cynical, naive, mater-of- fact, blasé tone.)

I wish I could tell you it was like: "My mother made dinner and my dad came home from work, and we all sat down, and we had a wonderful meal, and everybody laughed and talked."

But it wasn't. Dad's pattern was to stop off at the pool hall after work and have a few beers, shoot a few games of pool with the boys and not call, then turn up late for supper.

Scene: Walker drawing back an imaginary cue stick, fingers shaped into a good bridge.

Walker (VO): This usually had my mother really steaming, and they would escalate into a fight that made the evenings tense until it eventually broke into a screaming match with my mother at which point he would storm out of the house and further carouse and stay out until all hours with his buddies and then return in the middle of the night whereupon a screaming, door-slamming, shit-fit would ensue leaving us all cowering wide-eyed in our beds cursing her for not having the courage to leave him.

I wonder what he was so afraid of, made him want to run from it so much. Probably my mother! No, that's unkind. It's just old Father Night again out there grinning.

Scene: Walker looks away from watching baby, over towards the drapes on the patio door. Sound of the Boogeyman reggae becomes more prominent.

Walker (VO): Which is not to say that was the only thing I remember doing with him. Things were not all bad. He helped me with my algebra. I became a whiz at word problems, probably to please him, because it was something we did together.

I used to really like the wording of those word problems.

Two trains leave the station at the same time. One goes west at . . .

(pause)

Occasionally there would be a truce, sweetness even.

My mother would insist I go along with him to the pool hall, so he wouldn't get too drunk.

Walker (VO, *(singing in a twangy country-western voice*): Oh he loved to roll them balls down at the pool hall. He loved to go from dive to dive down the highway.

(Back to normal voice).

We'd go into cowboy dives or Mexican cantinas, and he was really good. He frequented some tough pool halls. He'd win money. He had a reputation around San Antonio for being a good pool player. Studying the configuration of molecules in chemistry must have helped his pool playing. He would play for 5, 10 and 20 or even 50 dollars which was a lot of money back then. There were some pretty rough looking characters, big beer guzzling Mexicans. My father and his boys.

FADE TO:

Scene: Opening front glass doors into cavernous inside of bowling alley, red, orange carpeting, and bright shiny lanes. Large electronic score monitors. Women with big beehive hairdos, guys in outrageous bowling shirts. Large pool room off to the left is behind glass. Thick with cigarette smoke. There are cowboys in tight jeans and guys with hair slicked back in that 50s style ducks.

Walker (VO): There was one pool hall in particular, Randy's Rodeo. It is this big bowling alley on Bandera Road, in San Antonio.

FADE BACK TO:

Scene: The Boogeyman from outside the apartment is now inside Walker's memory of this red-neck bowling alley. The Boogeyman is lumbering slowly, moving like a Sasquatch, a pile of leaves, a truly abominable snowman, among ashen-faced and increasingly hostile looking and more outraged bowlers, and barflies, and pool-hall louts.

Walker (VO): They would have killed a guy like that back at Randy's Rodeo.

Scene: A mob of rowdy Texas cowboys crowds closer and begins to hurl anything they can get their hands on at the alien in their midst: popcorn, beer cups, beer cans, hot dogs, bottles. As they do this, the light becomes stroboscopic so that just their gestures stand out stark, defined. They spit on him. The music becomes throbbing and dangerous in time with the strobe light. The Boogeyman is being harassed and pulled down by a pack of outraged Texas rowdies.

Walker (VO, *like a preacher*): They would have seen him as possessed by Satan. They would have felt secure, right that the Lord almighty had bestowed upon these good people the obligation and the power to smite the righteousness.

Scene: The mob fights among themselves to deliver a fist or a kick at the specimen. After the Boogeyman is knocked down by a smash from a boot, some Mexican guy starts stabbing him with a knife. A cowboy brings a shotgun out from under his duster and blasts away at the prone Yetti.

DISSOLVE TO:

Scene: Another quiet moment in the afternoon pool hall, not many people. Father takes fine ornate pool cue out of a felt-lined case and begins assembling it.

Walker (VO): He had his own cue stick, which he sometimes brought in with him, in a case. Sometimes he left it outside, because a lot of people wouldn't play you if you had your own cue.

Scene: (Loud CRACK of pool break echoing in a cavernous hall, thunderous reverberation, five bowling strikes at once, thunder outside the door)

Walker (VO): The CRACK of balls when he broke even in that cavernous den of iniquity could be heard across the pool hall on out the door and down the block.

Scene: Everybody in a large pool hall is casting quick, sly glances just for an instant at this short stocky man. He looks tough, like a Marine. Though very stocky, he moves fast, with grace and surprising speed.

Walker (VO): Everybody's head would turn to look at him. He could whip anybody in pool, like he could whip my mother around the dance floor. He was short but powerful, heavy but fast. He's not like me at all; I've towered over him since I was 13.

Scene: We hear loud twangy country western music.

Walker (VO): He was like this mechanic reaching in to make a small adjustment. Country western twang was coming out of the juke box, but what he heard was the music of the spheres.

Scene: We hear new age rushy, frothy, burbling space music.

Walker (VO): This was his own private universe, and he was like a god adjusting the spin or the influence of this ball on another. He just got all ***over*** that table, dominated it.

FADE BACK TO:

Scene: In kitchen again, Walker doing some martial arts moves using the "air pool cue" as a staff

Walker (VO): He moved around the table fast, intense, sinking ball after ball.

Walker (VO): Moving very fast all the while sizing up his next shot. He would never play me much because I wasn't ever a match for him. He would just take off and run the table.

If it was a friendly game, he would talk to me. He'd lean back in the stool next to me, touch his back to the wall, take a long pull on a Lone Star or a Bud, I think he liked Bud.

When he was bored and just wanted to play around, he would set up these multiple shots. He could actually do trick shots.

Scene: The large pool playing field is seen from the

perspective of the balls, sighting along the line of ball. Superimposed are various gages and protractors, rulers with ticks laid out on the green felt. For a moment the pool balls look like planets, and the table top becomes black starlit deep space. The music of the spheres rises. He shoots like the cue stick was a straight ray of sunlight or a laser beam shooting across space changing the position of planets through collision.

Walker (*quoting father's Voice)*: "It's all in the shape, Walker. This is a trine shot."

Scene: Back to Randy's Rodeo. Walker's large father is pointing things out, on a pool table—except the felt is black velvet, and it is like the universe in a box, with stars, and the pool balls are little bejeweled planets.

Walker's father: "You could have 3 planets in trine, 4 planets in square, and 6 planets in sextile. You usually didn't have to think about more than three balls at once."

Scene: Walker's father talking to young version of Walker in big pool hall of Randy's Rodeo.

Walker's father: "Now you and me, we have the same sign—Cancer. Right? Moon Children. So we could be in square like this."

Scene: Worlds colliding in deep space star field.

Walker (VO, *indicting internal monologue*): And he would set up 4 balls on the pool table. Bam! Crash! Moon collides with Jupiter, and down they all went into black holes.

DISSOLVE TO:

Scene: (Back in the kitchen talking to the baby)

Walker: Dancing and playing pool. He was like a little bull in a china shop that never broke a dish. He knew everything about pool: the boarders, the bounces, the turns, the music in his head, the crack of the balls.

FADE TO:

Scene: (Old car, young Walker with suitcase being dropped off on a highway. Young Walker hitchhiking.)

Walker (VO, *indicting internal monologue*): Soon as I could, I got out of there. When I finally got back to Canada, I was by myself at the age of fourteen.

One way or another, I made trips up to Canada every summer. I ran away from home for the first time when I was sixteen. I kept oscillating between Canada and the United States, the united states of hysteria. Oscillating between the pillars of male roles. Always needing to look for father figures.

Scene: Scenes of Canadian autumn farm land, very beautiful, bucolic. Little fluffy clouds floating by cast shadows on the fields. Lot of fiery orange red yellow maple trees.

Walker (VO): When I was eighteen, just out of high school, I got my first bachelor apartment in Montreal. It was 1967, the year of the EXPO when I visited Uncle Roddy on the farm in Canada. I had really long hair. I was helping my uncle. I was trying to find the right role model for how to live my life. I liked the idea of doing carpentry and being independent. I had always had a terrible time with authority.

CUT BACK TO:

Scene: In the kitchen Walker is pacing like a preacher on the pulpit, baby is drinking his bottle taking in the entertaining show with interest and smiling eyes.

Walker *(talking directly to baby in his carrier)*: We were *(pauses as if trying to remember)* trying to become more like wild men in those days.

FADE TO:

Scene: Good-looking, long-haired hippies hanging out in the woods. Just quick flashes, them playing hide and seek, larking, high. Like MTV rock band promo.

Father (VO): We were going to stand up to the machine that we saw grind down our fathers, and become these wild natural men with feelings. And you just got so much rejection from the men for having long hair.

FADE TO:

Scene: Scenes of long-hair person going through a suspicious small town. Fresh faced girls at the Dairy Queen, blushing and gawking at the long-hair boys, who have a defiant slouch in the way they walk down the main street. Matronly women with beehive hair look upon them with contempt.

Walker (VO): But my uncle understood!

When he saw my long hair for the first time, he looked at it, but he didn't say anything, he just accepted it. I could tell he wanted to say something, but he didn't.

I could see his mind working, and yet he did not reject me because of my hair. That felt really good.

I was working with him in the barn one day, and a look he gave me . . . well, something passed between us, a kind of acceptance I needed.

FADE TO:

Scene: Bright sun just after a rainstorm shining through the double-wide, open front doors of the barn.

Walker (VO): In the barn, there, as the sun was going down one afternoon, the bright summer warmth filtering through grass waving outside, beyond the opening of the double wide doors. The light came streaming into the barn like the ocean, pouring through the gaps between the boards, illuminating the roof beams overhead. The smell: old barn wood mixed with sawdust and turpentine, and a touch of cowpiss.

WIPE TO:

Scene: Small group of men, some fairly old, standing around a big, black, horse-drawn carriage being refurbished in the barn.

Walker (VO): We were rebuilding a hoosegow—a horse drawn carriage with black iron bars they used to haul people to jail. It was over a hundred years old.

We were going to enter it into the down town Main Street parade in Alexandria, Ontario, for EXPO. And a bunch of old guys, and city fathers, and just plain duffers passing the time, were standing around admiring the hoosegow. As the new trucks roared by on the highway, the conversation turned to old times and Canada's history and the boys were passing the bottle around, and the old men grinning and standing there like a bunch of big boys doing something their mother's and wives wouldn't like: drinking from this green half-pint bottle and passing it round the circle. And the next thing I know, they pass it to me! And my uncle gave me this look of smiling acceptance. And I took a drink and grinned at him, and it was like being admitted to a club: just this acceptance, that I was one of the men.

FADE BACK TO:

Scene: In the kitchen Walker pacing, entertaining baby.

Father *(talking directly to baby in his little seat)*: So why am I telling you about this hypothesis, about how we construct our character out of composites of our mother and father, or their substitutes? And what has that got to do with Father Night?

My uncle—the Good Father—gave me, through his acceptance, the blessing of innocence. My father—the Bad Father—gave me, through his rejection, the curse of emotional isolation.

Scene: The man and the baby are looking at each other, locked in mutual regard.

Father (*talking directly to baby in his little seat)*: This union of the family is like an onion. The father is the outer skin of the onion, and the mother is the primary care-giver at the center.

Scene: Father carefully picks up baby out of seat, gently nestles him over his shoulder onto a cloth to pat him gently on the back to burp.

Father (VO): The man feels excluded from that role. It's unmanly.

The father is there to break through into the outside world . . . he is this outer layer. Somehow his part in this is to be an image . . . a final staging ground, to get you ready and through which you must pierce to go out into the world.

A shadow, cold and remote as an interstellar pool game.

Scene: (Baby belches.)
Scene: Walker continues patting and goes over to the drapes at the large patio glass door and pulls them back a little bit to look out. We look across a garden of Easter lilies, tulips, and other cup-shaped flowers. The sound outside has stopped.

Walker (VO): *(talking directly to baby on his shoulder)*:

And we'll leave him digging in his garden . . . Learning the names of things . . . Pull some weeds. . . . Learn the names of the lilacs, the primroses, look deeply into their flowers, feel the softness of their petals, their most inner fuzziness. . . . Yes. Pull some weeds. Yes. Help it all along.

Help it ALL along, and know that he is a part and only a part of this ALL, too.

What about these flowers? How would Father Night see them?

Scene: Glides, dances gently with kid draped over his shoulder.

Walker (*as Father Night,* VO): My pretty little girls. Shaped, like the curvatures of space that informs it. It is not even what we see, but it is what shows up—the *forces* that shape it. The shape points to an invisible world, and it is pure trust.

O yes, my pretty little girls—Mother Earth bore you, but it is I, Big G, gravity shaping Father Time that holds you up. It is I, Negative Entropy that informs the shapes you take.

Scene: (Father playing as Father Time)

Walker (*as Father Night,* VO): Iris my dear, I have to say I like you best. Because you reflect the inward pull of the Hyperbola, the Black Hole at the center of this galaxy, the gravitational well. Unlike your exploding brothers, you implode.

And you have this cool lavender, almost metallic sheen about you, with the soft white throat.

Yes. Flowers remind me of the shapes of gravitational collapse.

(Scene: Walker, Father Night -Father Time, looks pensive, remorseful, full of feeling as he carries baby back up stairs to bed. The wind is making tree shadows dance on the wall, there is wan dim light.)

Walker (VO): You remind me of Beauty itself.

I want to hold you, to lift you up, protect you, pursue you, have you, guard you, destroy your enemies. Carry you along.

Scene: Carrying baby down the hall to bed.

Walker: (*singing softly to baby he is holding, draped over his shoulder)*: BO shan ... I caress...

(Scene: Setting sleeping baby down in bed. Looking over at the digital display on the clock reads 3 : 4 7)

Walker (VO): It's 3:47, the guy has gone way past his 15 minutes of fame. Maybe the Energizer batteries in his portable ran down. . . Social experiment to see how long it will take before the cops run him off. . . I'd like to have that tape.

Scene: Walker tucks baby in under covers and places his little bear beside him.

Walker: *(in a soft sing-songy voice to baby)*: Good night moon, (wherever you are).

Good night room, soft and warm, both here and there.

Good night bear, protects me from boogeymen everywhere.

Good night light, in the dark wall.

Good night door out to the hall.

Scene: Walker steals across the dimly-lit bedroom and looks out the window. The music has stopped. He peers out the window. We see the same intersection, empty.

Walker (VO): Even the Boogeyman has to bow to the rain.

Good night, Night, good night Pall,

Good night world, beyond it all.

Scene: Walker at his own bed, lifting covers and sliding beneath them

Wife's voice: *(sleepily)* What was that noise?

Walker: Oh, some street-person off his meds. With a boom box.

Wife's voice: *(sleepily)* Everything okay?

Scene: She is turned away from him. He snuggles down into bed, in a spoon.

Walker: Yep. . . Good night wife, light of my life. *(humorously)*

Mmmmm. Nothing like nice warm buns.

Scene: Camera on man and woman in bed, heads on pillow above covers. Camera view moving around dark room, pulling back slowly looking at them from the ceiling. Camera view moves back and forth a little, looking at them from different angles, then pulls back further, to see the house from above outside. Then pulls up quickly to see the house in neighborhood, and neighborhood in city, and city in state and state in country. Camera view zigzags and moves off into the star fields of space.

Father Night

A Blue Moon in August

A few days after the flight back from a family vacation, Walker wrote a letter about it to his brother Roux. Walker and Sam and their wild child, Shredder the Micro-hellion, had spent a week at a Club Med in Ixtapa, Mexico. (On the return trip, Walker had thrown out his back carrying Shredder in a backpack on the long walk through and around the airport corridors to Los Angeles customs—oddly a radio in their backpack had turned on from the jostling and began playing "Everybody is a dancing machine." And, Walker had started a new job, with all the stress *that* brings.)

It had been good to get away. Walker was not the type to take vacations, but Sam was. She required them. And even though Walker ate some wrong food at the sumptuous spread Club Med puts out and got tourista, and in spite of the fact that they were too incapacitated by the heat to get around much, (the rooms had air-conditioning) and even though it rained almost every day, the trip had been enlightening. The disappointments were minor compared to the blue moon dream he had on the night of the second full moon in August. And on the next night after that, just walking around the place and recording the jungle sounds, he had one of those transcendental moments you get in life. In the letter, he wrote:

Dear Roux,

Sorry to have been so long getting back to you. Tried to call a couple of times. I started a new contract job at Visa doing a model of their network. It is all interactive on the computer, no paper. It is a great project, I can't believe I am so lucky. Been hanging out all year getting a little unemployment waiting for the right gig to come along. I have made it part of my work to learn something about 3D perspective drawing, too, because it is a good way to visualize, and it solves the problems of where to click on the interactive model. Yay!

Me and Sam and the Wild Child made a trip to Ixtapa Mexico. Sam is so good at saving money, made me save even out of the unemployment checks—which, believe me my brother, are *small.* Man, I needed the change. I've really become a very boring, stay-at-home guy, writing all the time, trying to save some of my art from oblivion. (Having a kid makes you want to have something to say to them.) My greatest expense is this little studio office I'm in, writing you this letter. (I got out of the cubicle box into an office box). In a house 3 blocks from home. Home, it feels funny to say that, can't quite believe it; I'm always on the verge of bolting, but I'm hanging in. Anyway, it was one of these charter deals, to a Club Med with day care. All travel, housing, and food provided. Couldn't put together a more attractive (cheaper) package. It was beautiful down there, right on the ocean. I love swimming in the ocean. Sam is a pool person—I didn't go in the pool once—but Ahhh, the warm Pacific. All that bright color during the day; and I loved listening to the crickets and cicadas at night. Went out and taped them on the August blue moon. It rained almost every day, and I ate the wrong food, so I was barfing and shitting myself all one night, but that purge was part of the experience, too, and I might have seen God in the bottom of the toilet bowl and didn't die, but laid around for several days. Besides that, somehow being on the cramped plane on the way back and lifting luggage and Shredder threw my back out, but it wasn't a bad vacation. I'd go again. It's a real frontier down there. Ixtapa is near Zihuatanejo. I was down there 20 years ago with a woman I was living with at the time. Back then we were following in the steps of Timothy Leary. Man, it has really changed. What a frontier town. There are swarms of workers building all this federally developed tourist mecca: high rise condos, new roads, marinas and shopping malls, in that labor-intensive, stone and earth moving way the Mexicans do things. But we mostly stayed at the Club Med village of condos which were air-conditioned as we were too bunged up to move much and too incapacitated by the heat to get around; but it was beautiful. If I was a young man with a big hammer and a truck, I'd go down there and take on that land. Grab a piece of it, for it is wild—all that bright light and color, swarming with life. As it is up here sometimes, I think, in this computer world, I feel like I have become a geek. All the time up in my head. All the time sitting in front of a computer. I've never had back trouble, and it scares me. You are smart to be doing physical work, it has lots of benefits. This office I have now, there are just paths between the piles of books and papers. I have accumulated tickets which are rapidly maturing in value because I haven't been keeping up with the mail.

I had this amazing experience down in Mexico, man. It came after this weird dream I had on the night of the Blue Moon. I think it has to do with what I was working on in my own writing lately. And with this family I am in.

I have been thinking/working on this story called *Church of the Coincidental Metaphor* for a long time. It is about these guys in Austin who buy Mexican radio time for a religious parody show that they broadcast on those million-watt border bandit stations all the way up through the American bread basket. Part of the story is, the guys get a wild hair and make a trip down to Mexico to actually *see the station*, whose call letters are XAOS, outside of Guernalavaca. So on this journey to Ixtapa, I got a lot of imagery for the story. The boys drive down dirt roads past white-washed buildings some of which have eroded corners. A sign painted on a *Farmacia* is eroding, and the adobe lath behind it starts to appear. They come to the radio station outside of town. It is ochre-colored with a red tile roof and orange Satillo tiles on the patio. There are little inlaid green and blue tiles in the top and bottom corners.

Anyway, on the night of the Blue Moon, Wed. Aug. 31, 1992—the second full moon in August—I had this dream. The dream had our family when we were growing up in San Antonio. I guess this was right around the time you were born 'cause we, the sisters and I, were still real little. Somehow we got this gas station to live in. It was mostly wall-to-wall, roll-up, glass doors across the front of it. It was well off the highway, a big wide highway in Texas. (Actually, I recognized the gas station as part of all the gas stations I have worked in around San Antonio and part of the Dairy Queen on Bandera Road.)

Anyway, in the dream, people didn't always recognize that the gas station had been converted to housing, and they would drive up with the lights of their car peering in like eyes. And we were in there! Being looked at! It was such a weird place to live. The hoses, and racks, and the hydraulic lift platform were still there. Our father mounted a little platform on the lift and put a baby grand piano he got from his mother on top of it. And he would make himself rise up into the air while playing the piano and singing *Summertime* from Porgy and Bess.

Next door to the gas station home was a huge warehouse. A big white building with no windows on any sides except for the front; it took up the whole block. (I recognized later it was Randy's Rodeo, and it was side by side with the Dairy Queen, although in reality they are on opposite sides of the street).

There was something awfully peculiar about that warehouse. There was a constant sputter and poof of energy about it. To say straight out what I think it was? The building was some kind of inter-regional exchange of a vampire expressway. In which strange beings went in and out of the corners of things. And you could observe it . . . like, it was projected on the inside of the wall. Like it was a billowing electronic pinball video game. At least *I* could see it.

I know it sounds weird. First thing, maybe they weren't vampires, I don't think they actually had such a malicious intent. But the people in the building had these awful pasty-faced looks about them, and they all had a 5-o'clock shadow. Some of the men had dirty pony tails and looked untrustworthy. And I say pinball machine or video game, there was all this running around and movement of light and color. Like driving through Las Vegas fast in an open car. Only it was on a screen and pushing off the edges of the screen because the screen was wrapped around the corners of something. Well basically, there were just faces that zoomed up and disappeared around a corner, like they were goin' down a drain. Then another face, or maybe it was the same face—altered—would take its place. I got the sense that when I was a kid I had spent a lot of time sitting out there at the gas station and watching the comings and goings-on inside the building, it was like I could kind of see through the wall.

One day, in the dream, I decided to investigate this building. It was like a cochlea, and there were these rings of beads of beings circling around it. People were being converted and sent out—hammered out—into the world.

"I'm not supposed to see this!" I heard my inner voice screaming inside my head.

Anyway, that's all I remembered. But now as I start trying to interpret it for you, I have to go back to the context in which it occurred. A dream is like a box within a box. A story that is aware of itself, that comments on itself. So, anyway, the context. What has coincidental metaphors got to do with it you might ask. Coincidental metaphors are like name freaks: the fact that Lincoln had a secretary named Kennedy and Kennedy had a secretary named Lincoln. And both presidents were assassinated! Coincidental metaphors are paranoid schizophrenic insights into the way the world works. Probably totally wrong-headed. (Why am interested in this?) I think it has great potential for humor. And the radio thing, it is about voice moving at the speed of light through the air and touching down on anybody who has a receiver. Lot of poetry in that. Radio is like the Soul emanating, expanding out — invisible and touching everyone at the speed of light. I'd like to get this story right someday. There is so much to learn.

But the dream; I'm trying to analyze it. A dream presents a person's concerns in a landscape where an experience is just at the edge of human understanding. I 'know' where the imagery comes from. It was like when we were kids being in the Bandera drive-in movie in our pajamas, running around the car. Dad would let me and the sisters out of the car, (you must have been a babe in arms, about the age of my kid now) and I was the oldest so I was in charge. On those warm Texas nights, you could run up to the front where they had some of those steel lawn chairs, and there were swings and a merry-go-round, and it was really something to be on the merry-go-round, goin' round and round and to look up onto the huge drive-in screen at the skewed angle, or to be swinging low and letting your feet get sucked up high into the starry sky overhead, (this was back in the 50s when there wasn't so much pollution) and looking back up the drive-in screen at the strange black and white images upside down.

One aspect of the Church of the Coincidental Metaphor is that is seeks to use parody, satire, and even blasphemy to push aside the other religions and make a place for itself. It also believes humor is at the bottom of the spiritual. Its symbol is a picture of a closed finite universe from mathematics called the Klein bottle. This is a bottle whose neck rises up out of itself, then curves back and flows back inside itself. Thus what gets poured out comes back in. It is a symbol made to supplant the cross, that dolorous image of a man who tried to help people love each other hung out to dry; or more abstractly of the way our rational mind is always having to cleave space into the horizontal and vertical (the diachronic and synchronic) and analyzing everything and itself out of the picture. The recirculating universe model instead of the analytical cross. The cochlea is a representation of this as well as the heart and lungs.

Man, this is wild. Here I am talking to my brother about a dream that included our family, a dream that came about from an artistic quest for a symbol of a religion that poured back in upon itself through the languages of imagery. And it comes to me, the Klein bottle is about the dream's desire to be perfectly fulfilling, like the way nature pours what comes out of itself back into itself. It's a picture of natural fractal feedback across dimensions, a dance before your eyes, a subliminal opera among one's conscious, subconscious, and superconscious folding and rotating and sliding into and out of one human form into another and into your own true animal identity, even into and out of spirit and matter.

But as it was, down in Mexico on this family trip me and Sam and Wild Bill were on, getting sick those couple of days, where I got purged, and it's raining a lot, and being as I quit drinking coffee making me really sensitive, except I slept a lot which is great because I stayed with the wee lad, and we took naps together in the afternoons while Sam went to her aerobic classes, and I stayed with him at night while Sam went out to shows because I don't really care to watch a bunch of actors jumping around. I just didn't feel all that good until near the end, when I did some body surfing and took a sailing lesson. I learned a great move from the locals: when playing in the surf, standing with your back to an incoming wave, when the wave comes in, leap up in the air, and let it take your legs out from under you and you just slide backwards down the back-side of the wave as it moves on through. It is like doing an arching pole vaulting maneuver. Really fun. The little local Mexican kids at the beach loved it when I started doing this backover maneuver with them.

Well, I'm just rambling on now, better get this off.

Love,

Walker

On the last night before they were to leave Ixtapa and after the dream, Walker strolled around the grounds making an audio tape of the sounds and the space. He had a way of curling up a tiny microphone back on its lead and inserting one in each of his ears! So then the recording used the acoustics of his headspace to give a binaural rendering of the 3D locations of the sounds in the space. He now put on the earphones and played the tape recording. He listened to the recording he had made and the memory of the idea of home, of being part of *family,* flooded in. Walking around the grounds of the Club Med on the hot tropical full moon night had been one of those moments when your life comes into focus, and you just kind of know that this is where you are supposed to be.

He was walking by himself, with the DAT. Marveling at the headroom of the Digital Analog Tape recorder. He was picking up the waves coming ashore on the beach below. And when the waves receded, he could hear the wall of cricket and cicada song rising. He could hear people beyond normal hearing range in the night clubs and bars talking and glasses tinkling. Then, when the waves rolled in below, these sounds were drowned out in the sucking-slide sound of receding ocean white noise over shore stones. Everywhere the bushes on the well-kept grounds were swaying in a dance, doing that white-noise shhh-shee-tittlescree that they do in the wind. The gaslight torches with warm flames were flickering against peach and pink and ochre colored walls. These were the inverse of the day's green jungle fan against the blazing blue sky and earth colors in a bright clime.

The place was like the Alamo. Except the thick adobe ivy-draped walls were warm colored. The Spanish effect was enhanced by lighting alcoves and niches and arches. Huge ceramic urns stood silently beside portals like fat guards. Lights strung through trees focused the attention on what is being illuminated, magnolia trees lit from below made them look like gothic or rococo altars at a medieval Church of Natural Philosophy with openings and mouths for a cathedral effect. The walkway beneath his feet was dappled in a leafy pattern from being lit from above. You could see luminaire itself because the lanterns from which the light was emitted had frosted, sandblasted glazing.

And when Walker looked back at the little bright-colored green door of their condo room, the velvety, soft, diffused, off-white rays of luminous moon-glow coming down from a perfectly round full moon magnified in the tropical sky pierced the layers of the space like it was a glass box, to illuminate boxes within the box.

Inside the outside box was one man, walking 'neath the full moon out away, past the edge of the complex to the slide of the sea. Inside the inside box was one woman and a child (who was the union of the man and woman).

The man himself was of such a union. And he imagined the two of them in there, his wife and his child, in a tender light, mother and child together, locked in each other's loving gaze. And he thought: Yes, this is the definition of good. He continued, moving slowly at the pace of the regular slow sea. He felt as perceptive as water seeking its own level. Moving down the hill, he felt like a falling wave, crashing in on the shore from beyond. And looking the other way you could see beyond: past the ramparts of the hotel, to the indistinct mountains, making up the edge of things.

The clouds in the distant night sky were illuminated from behind by the moon which had gone over the horizon. It made the clouds look like mushrooming shadows cast up by the trees, as if the trees were standing in the way of a light that came from below, from within the earth. This was the night side of things, where the trees had learned how to be from the ancient clouds.

HiT MoteL Press

www.hitmotel.com

These books can be ordered from any book seller or on-line, are deeply discounted on Amazon, and Barnes& Nobles. Check www.hitmotel.com for selections and recordings.

Boho Novels

The "Little House on the Prairie" Trilogy:

Cultivating the Texas Twister Hybrid, a portrait of the artist as a weed gardener (1998) ISBN 0-9655842-0-8 $20.00

The Secret of the Cicadas' Song, a peyote trip in poetry and prose (1998) ISBN 0-9655842-1-6 $20.00

Knight of a 1000 eyes, about Tai Chi, movement, Laban, and the I Ching (2002) ISBN 0-9655842-2-4 $25.00

others:

The Punctual Actual Weekly, about the life and times of a small mimeograph literary rag centered around artists living in a Berkeley warehouse and the Amphictionic Theatre ISBN 0-9655842-8-3

The Church of the Coincidental Metaphor, youthful adventures in Mexican radio

Novels: The "My Years of Apprenticeship at Love" Sextet:

Sex is the Anti-gravity of Metamorphosis, tales of romance and despair hitchhiking in North America. ISBN 0-9655842-9-1

The Indigenous Tribesmen of Neverland Bohemian life in Austin slacker enclaves. ISBN 0-9655842-7-5 $20.00

Dolores Park, Texan joins a California Tantric Buddhist commune (2001) ISBN 0-9655842-3-2 480 pages. $25.00

Seeing throught the Spell of Transference A cab driver's journal of psychotherapy. ISBN 0-9655842-4-0

A Blue Moon in August, about marriage and children late in life. (2005) ISBN 0-9655842-5-9

Thoughts on Vacation, a father is raised by his child and is enlightened by mortality. (2005) ISBN 0-9655842-6-7

Check into HiT MoteL @www.hitmotel.com for cover art, interactive Table of Contents, e-book sample chapters, recordings and other mindware.

http://www.hitmotel.com **HiT MoteL Press**

The "Little House on the Prairie" trilogy

The "My Years of Apprenticeship at Love" sextet

in progress

A Blue Moon in August

A Blue Moon in August, is a comedy of manners about marriage and children late in life. It is the 5th novel in the "My Years of Apprenticeship at Love sextet" about Walker Underwood, now a bohemian information worker in Berkeley and Silicon Valley who meets and marries and becomes a father late in life and suddenly.

The story is told from the perspective of both the man and the woman as they come to embrace their commitment to each other. Shifting between third and first person narrative within their stories, we enter fantasy and dreams or see the characters from outside through a 'bookmovie'.

It is a novel in the form of their emotional memories and creative experiences—the man's as he struggles with the decision to marry, and finds the male role model of marriageability and becomes a father—and the woman's as she liberates herself from her family to start her own.

One chapter—The Prowess of Kong, presents the great hippie dream of group marriage in a Tantric Buddhist commune as a contrast to traditional marriage. Another chapter—Urban Angst at the 7-11 in 2019, a cyberpunk sci-fi, presents a man's fear of the future and coming to rely on his wife.

A Blue Moon in August, is a hilarious picture of a new father undergoing the spell of motherhood and struggling to maintain his sense of self and grow with it.

$25.00 Literature/ Cyberpunk/ Parenting Romance

www.ingramcontent.com/pod-product-compliance
Lightning Source LLC
LaVergne TN
LVHW091052080826
845145LV00002B/719

9780965584258